T0095128

Sunshine State

Sunshine State

A Novel Of Sorts

ASAF RUBINA

Order this book online at www.trafford.com
or email orders@trafford.com

Most Trafford titles are also available at major online book retailers.

© Copyright 2011 Asaf Rubina.
All rights reserved. No part of this publication may be reproduced, stored in a retrieval
system, or transmitted, in any form or by any means, electronic, mechanical, photocopying,
recording, or otherwise, without the written prior permission of the author.

Printed in the United States of America.

ISBN: 978-1-4269-5380-4 (sc)
ISBN: 978-1-4269-5381-1 (e)

Trafford rev. 01/06/2011

 www.trafford.com

North America & International
toll-free: 1 888 232 4444 (USA & Canada)
phone: 250 383 6864 ♦ fax: 812 355 4082

To my friends and family, your continued concern and interest has been the outmost form of salutation. Your kind feedback has weighed heavily on the influence of this release.

This book has played an important role in my life.

Sunshine State

I. A God Damn Mess

II. Blonde Glow

V. Elements Of Disaster

VI. Before The End Is Carried

Sometimes it's hard to pretend that a line hasn't been crossed.

I. A God Damn Mess

SHARDS

At Mika Mango's, Savage and I go posh out while I order the usual Bistec a la Mexicana with extra jalapenos and that guac that I love so well that always seems to bathe in a pool of lime. It's a plain day, and a dark one if you may, and the intent is to make it out to Sashi Bar where the game is on and from what I hear, just the total babe rally. Remember, the potential in this town has indeed dwindled over the past few years, and hanging out by the pool has turned into being cooped up in the kitchen cooking up the grind for the tweezer locals on a rush, but. A bunch of fucking brush-off dwibble nuts with a weak stomach for the hard kish. Savage orders the Burrito Porque, which isn't really even a burrito, but more of a *chimichanga* and I nudge in approval even though the worm doesn't come with chips, happens to be double fried and drenched in a very watery white queso, and is pretty much a complete and total waste of his six-fifty. Savage mentions something about the fight last night and how the girls were trying to get some attention the whole time we were at Chuck's and how I just seemed too fucked to mind, but I fade him out through my shades and focus my ears on the girlies of the stoop (especially the blonde one, *yes, the blonde one*) seated next to us who seem to be getting really pissed that their server hasn't brought out their side of sour on a dime. "No worries ladies, these guys are good. *I come here all the time,*" saying in a smug fashion, although I can tell the friend is real creeped out in my attempts to ease their lingering frustration. She seems shocked that I would even dare to approach their presence out here on this patio on this shit-storm of a July afternoon and I can tell she's thinking *doesn't he see, like, how hot my friend is?* or *we've seen the likes of you at the midnight falloffs, but like, we're not fucking now, are we pretty boy?* or *watch out we've got pedicures to get* and just then I notice for the first time that my phone has been vibrating on the table sliding smoothly into the drop of salsa my neglected bite dribbled on the table. I also recognize that the blonde one is giggling and acknowledges that she, in fact, is way more appealing than her double douche bag friend here and can sense that I too, recognize this very important detail. *Don't you see that we, are like, better than you?* I pull out a cool pack of smokes and ask Savage for a light when there's a sudden blonde interruption "are those Camels?" and I say yes to which she replies "they're like $7.50 a fuckin' pack now," to which I begin to establish a certain level of self defense, and think if this total skag-rag nut-sling even mentions getting a puff she can well bowl her fucking brains out cause these yins are not too be bummed, but whored for, but I do think it's kind of hot that she's got a fowl little mouth on her and I start to think of things I'd like to put in that gear, working on a soft orifice, grabbin' on the jaw, mind you. I notice the phone continues to vibrate and I'm like *whaaat is it?!* as I begin to blow puffs of smoke towards her friend's direction. This doesn't last long before they depart in frustration of sitting next to a complete asshole and not getting the shit they ordered from Manuel with the sour. The food finally arrives and I ask Manuel what happened to the girl's dairy sauce to which he replies *what girls?* and I laugh and Savage laughs and we all just completely rally up because we know who we are and how we feel and what that means to us, and deep down inside, it's all we can truly give a fuck about. My phone continues to vibrate and just as I'm about to answer it, more food gets here, and before you know it I'm done stuffing my face and Manuel asks if we need anything else and I say two shots of hot cuervo, and he asks if we want them chilled, to which we don't reply and my phone keeps vibrating, and I finally just can't take it anymore and decide to answer it.

The Runner

He told me there was no such thing as writer's block, as if some concrete still is enforced deep inside us, since earlier I had so much I wanted to say. When you're done, you just keep on writing and when you write you think of all the words you are putting together and the way you are spelling them and how when you look up you have made so many mistakes that you just want to stop but you don't and keep going and you write and you write until your fucking fingers fall off and then the night is day and everyone is awake and you're still trashed from the night before, melting into one, nestling in the sun and have made no real segue way in designing any form of connection between anything you've written.

It's quite funny really. The in out in out of the computer screen has brought my eyes to tender and now that I begin to stare blankly at the melting bulb as my brain begins to boil as my thoughts start to blur, I fall from my seat and collapse only to awaken in a dreary still that reminds me of everything that is my past and what it was that brought me here and now that I look to what I write I startle at the thought of this media and how the outlet is an escape when nothing is on the tv and the ability to dismiss myself from the illusory that is the very common form of our day and night and find comfort in this commotion of dreary thoughts and steady footprints. I know how we were talking and how you brought me back to size and how when we were outside we were laughing up a storm and you were rambling off again because you were heavy on the dosage, but I would wait and anticipate your return to point, and even though I know it never comes I still enjoy the entertainment and is it past or is it present and are we talking or are we faking and are you here or are you there and how is it that when we're together that you still seem so far away? It's been so long now.

It's been so long.

Susana...

But it is night now. Fangs are being purged out of my tight, pink, tinkling gums and as the skin beneath my lip begins to rip, I await your return because when you get here you are either one of us or you are none of us and you will either live or die eternally and as my point reaches a peak I begin to calm and find comfort in dismissing imagination and incorporating the common form into text and how when the words are put together you can actually find yourself and begin to truly feel.

Are you still reading this? Are you finding pleasure in this? Can we commute on this? Is there any joy I can bring to you in this? I'll bring you buttered biscuits and crumpets and laugh until it is lunch and we are at the patio drinking margaritas and the game is on and the air is cool and the night is young and just the thought of us going out together later kills me and oh all the fun that tonight is going to bring is enough for me to ease. But now my cuts begin to bleed and as I think of you again I am dismissed and the bell rings and everyone is out the door on Wednesday since it's early day and everyone is gone and I am left alone not only to once again miss the bus back, and now I just *can't* get back so I head towards the track and I'll just keep running and I'll just have to stay and then, I think, is this what he meant to keep writing?

And like an aneurism it hits you in the face. The writer is reborn from a serious shock of lurid thought, emerging from the goo of after-birth. Awaking to a new life. How could this be? How is it possible that a lone stranger in a room cannot compose his feelings into a cohesive work? Work that would contribute to the understanding of his intentions. To the understanding of his reasons. Work that would identify his philosophy. Who would be able to understand him otherwise? In what manner could he possibly be trying to present himself where he could not possibly be any clearer?

It all starts from this dream I had where I was grinding my teeth, and I mean really grinding them. Like, lower jaw, you know the main four in the front bottom, going right between the two choppers on the top, and I mean just going into them. Like, to the bleedings gums. No hurt or pain or anything. Just knowing that I'm grinding the shit out of my teeth and living with it, *like it's this thing I do...* making the choppers disappear like the boys did down in Smith Lane.

I wake up left in a bit of a loss, dismissing the horrid nature of the dream, and just then I recall how I once heard that you only remember about two or three dreams from a series of a thousand plenty a night, and all you can recall from these short few is a light motif or concept or a slight reminder that triggers the memory, but either way, this was the one thing I remembered and I woke up realizing that I was in my very own urn. The nightmare within the dream. I had died due to bloodshed. How truly fucked. Had reality set in the dream world I would have torn down in defeat towards the expense of the dental co-pay.

When I brushed my teeth that morning, I was entirely aware of my mouth and quickly became alerted to the mechanics of the human figure and how it manages to provide, so involuntarily, the process of making us behave in the manners that we do. It does this in disregard of our feelings. Arms making sure poor teeth are brushed. Dick makes sure good pussy gets fucked. The human chemistry is designed in a way that will allow it to remain active and persistent. That's why blood cells repair themselves. It is the individual's pursuit of destruction regarding their physical shape that causes the body's drive to dwindle, somehow augmenting the chemistry of the human form. Obese existers, be gone! If you think about the kneecap and how beautiful of a thing it really is and how mysterious the chemistry of the cartilage is, I mean, wow, that is just some beautiful shit there. Just where exactly do you get the balls to detriment it with your weight? They say I'll burn in hell for my sins, but what about the gluttons? Do they not consume and destroy their own temples like those of us who slay? But we were never anything like that, of course…

I brushed so hard my gums bled, and I liked it.

My feet stuck to the bathtub and the bathroom was freezing.

And by now my heart is beating so hard that it almost hurts to write this. I mean, I am straining for the keyboard scrunching my eyes to focus on this blazing screen and I hope that my phone does not ring again, wishing it is her. It is time to get started here.

THE WORKS

We were all trash and Pam was a total lush. A complete and outmost wreck, mind you. I had my dick out, and she was sucking it, yeah, that much I can remember. But who was that over there? Was it Carl?

Carl had the tendency to be the real pervert. I often found him hiding in the closet when Pam would come over to rub. And this wasn't just in the middle of Saturday night brooha's, mind you - I'm talking about a straight up middle-of-the-fucking-day-bonanza. What would he be doing there? Would he anticipate our entrance to the room? How truly fucked!

We had "Booty Beach Babe Blowout!" at the house last week and it was a total rape fest of last years' "The Real Deal Party For Real" party which was a total disgraceful cockfest and fag hang and the theme was a total bore to motherfuckin' begin with. We had six kegs with five backups out to start, fifteen gallons of hunch punch (jungle juice, depending on the district), ten to fifteen gallons or so of Jim Beam, and 1,354 visitors. The front door was torn off the hinges by ten and the fridge had managed to find its way into the living room, laying on its side with all the contents (jelly, red wine, mustard, and other assorted jars) shattered on the carpet that were mashed into it deeply. The house, you can say, was officially totaled. But, needless to say, twenty-one of us got laid that night and it was borderline - a total orgy. We only had three bedrooms at the house, but when all the guys heard about the party they came from all over the state and all the dudes from out of town and up the coast with all the girls from every corner showed up at our stoop. The living room opened up displaying a beachfront theme with real sand even. In the morning, all the buggers were just laying in their own filth on top of one another. At this point forty-two people were in the main room laying buttass naked. I even counted for the keepsake and snapped the photo. Everyone else had gone home at around 8:15 the next morning, way after Christina, the milfy next door neighbor, called the cops when she found Carl beating off in her backyard with my copy of the September 2005 issue of INTL *Club*, which featured Janine on the front cover. Figures. He was Tara's boyfriend, who for some reason would just hang around the house sometimes, even when she wasn't around. At first we didn't make much of it, but now that I think about it, a certain word must be said to Tara about these politics. Needless to say, I never got the magazine back.

Yeah, so Tara was this real hippie chick always throwing a fuck towards my way and always paying the bills a month before, but just the fact of her having sex with that Carl bozo would drive me limp and I would rise and leave the room, shutting the door violently behind me mid-lay. I knew she was a total freak when she started bringing guys home that she was chatting up with on the internet, be it the future or not, I've had enough of their negligence. Pam and I couldn't even get a descent wank in since Carl was behind the door, breathing heavily. I never agreed to let Tara give him a key to the house, but who was going to watch her cat? Sure as the professor wasn't going to be me.

Summer days in December were always the total fuck up.

I decide to wait for the poor fucker to get home. This time around I've come to terms with losing the old mind and plan on terrorizing the little shit and getting into that face of his from start to finish for the maniacal, perverted, selfish ways of his demeanor.

This guy.

The total fuck off.

Tara had left earlier in the afternoon and told me Carl was going to be by later to watch Darla the Cat. This was just perfect since Pam was on her way over and we were going to watch that Tenacious D movie where they go and find the pick of destiny that's part musical and part laugh riot and the whole thing is basically a beat off comedy sesh. Not to mention, I had a hard on beyond erection and my cock was so stiff that if she didn't loosen the tension soon enough I was going to have to beat off to that new website I found last weekend when Ben came over after the bars and was sleeping on the floor and I was jerking off over him and cummed on his sleeping bag.

Pam gets in just before three o'clock and we rush to my room and undress and she's not wearing any panties and I'm absolutely loving it even though I'm a huge thong freak, and before I can even get her down she already has my dick in her mouth and she spits on it over and over and over again until it is wet as fuck and I say "geez, lady!" and as she gets on top of me she exposes her bare cunt and I slap the piece, and we start to laugh and before you know it I go inside and five minutes after that we're already in the living room eating nachos and ice cream watching *Sparks,* and I'll be damned if you can find me one good thing better than the midday lay.

Halfway into the movie Pam blacks out, too tired from the in-n'-out motion of it all. I finish off the nachos after reheating them to melt the cheese again, and then head to my room letting her dose off on the couch until later when we'll probably go at it again. I want to do it to the new Suffokate album I bought last weekend when I was all cracked out, and spent over $300 or so at CD Universe. I anticipate that with her habits she'll be out for the majority of the night and head into the garage, where I reach into my toolbox and start sharpening a knife, thinking about Carl, knowing full well that he is going to be here soon. I grab the machete with the wooden handle and bring it back and forth on the tool I got from the gift shop at Dunbey Adventures (a total skag local joint found right next door to the paintball field we used to go to every weekend that deals exclusively in the maintenance of historic hand held weapons) and as I put the big fucker down and grab the hand held pieces one by one, I sharpen the tools to a point with a cheeky grin and a toothy smile going from ear to ear drooling with anticipation. *The things I'll do to this fucker, the things I'll do...* My imagination begins to run rampant, and I'm seeing all in red and blood is just pouring from the walls, floating down the hallway making its way all throughout the house, and just as I walk back in through the door, I hear the chime ding from the living room.

And there he is!

Guest of Honor arrives and I open the door and he already eyeballs Pam on the couch trying to sneak a peak at her puss that's been hanging out since before, as she's wearing a short denim skirt that has risen up well above her thigh. I hold the machete to my back and let him enter before me. Lips shut, cheeky grin present, eyes WIDE open. *Come through, saaahhh...*

Not two seconds in before I violently slash his back.

I can see the gauging wound on his back begin to stain his shirt blood red as he crawls on all four, and for some reason, I have a moment of clarity big enough to realize that I've just completely lost it. I see his hands spread apart as he pulls himself on the floor beneath him and the webbing between his fingers is just so white knuckle tight and is now stretched apart with pressure, that I just have to go grab a pair of scissors and chop them apart. Giggling as I head into the backroom since I don't have a pair handy, I can feel my chest about to burst from extreme heart rate. As I hop over Guest of

Honor, who won't be going anywhere anytime soon, I spy a shot at the wall mirror and realize a huge splash of blood has sprayed across my shirt. I rub my index finger into my shirt and put it to my mouth and taste it like it's that last line of coke after the all night gig and I rub it deep, deep, deep into my gums. I can hear him begin to moan in the hall, as he crawled quite a ways by now, getting close into the room I came from with the scissors, and as I rush back I cringe, as I can see Pam starting to wake.

It doesn't take long for everything to fall apart and before you know it Pam is screaming off her beating lungs so loud and so hard that I have to tie her up to ensure everyone's safety, and as I throw her over my shoulder, she just continues to shriek and starts slamming hard on my back, begging for me to let her go and even though I want to, I just can't. *I can't.* Who knows where she can run off to? Even though I love the cunt, it's safe to say I have no inclination for common form and all behavior at this point is well beyond repair.

I take the two of them to the garage outside and stuff a big pair of black cotton dress socks into Pam's mouth as I rope her tightly to a wooden chair. I blindfold her face since I don't want her to see the crazy shit about to go on and as I give her a distant kiss on the cheek, I eyeball Guest of Honor, who is sweating bullets by now, and before you know it, he has lost so much blood from the enormous gash I inflicted on him earlier in the living room, that he passes out. I really wish Pam could share this with me, but after being with her for close to the last three years now, I know full well how the girl would behave in a scam. Best to not let things get too complicated.

I leave the room, only to return from the driveway with a full container of gas. I'm not planning on torching the fucker, but I do think the stench of gas will resuscitate his senses up a bit. As I begin to splatter him top to bottom, left to right, he starts to wiggle. Wiggles like a little worm. And just then I think about that scene in *Reservoir Dogs,* where Mr. Blonde ties the cop who he's taken hostage from the failed robbery who kept on saying he didn't know nothing about no setup, and as I go to the stereo and blast Johnny Truant's *Death Rides*, I just start punching his brawny, pale face with both hands, alternating in a sick rhythm until his cheeks are black and blue (purple like a plum, actually) and his skin begins to tear.

He has closed his eyes for the better part of the whole thing, and started mumbling prayers for whatever reason, and I just can't take his denial of the scenario, so I take a pair of scissors nearby and cut off his eyelids. His prayers suddenly morph into screams and he is twisting on the floor like a cockroach that just got smashed but is somehow still alive. It's then that I use the opportunity to take a pair of pliers and go to his wide-open mouth to rip his two front teeth out, and all that's left is a giant gap between the other two fangs. It's then that I lean in to tell him that if he doesn't shut his mouth and stop screaming, I'll slit his throat.

CUTTING YOUR FUCKING FACE APART

In a dream shot in aerial view, we're both caught driving down Lane Way and I'm going north but you're going south and we're both in the same lane heading straight for one another, and I refuse to move and I know your stubborn ways, so I just toss it all in the air and wait for us to clash and as the two cars collide going over a hundred, we make eye contact as we crash and you cringe, all while I smile and flash a quick wink from the other side, and before you know it we both fly through each other's windshield and my face is torn apart from the glass and my left arm is over there, my legs are over here and my whole midsection is just numb, and I cannot hear or see or feel a single thing and as I come to terms with my paralysis, I begin to laugh and this is what causes me to wake.

I rise from the bed while you still sleep and go piss apart my brains out. I lift the seat up and the urine hits the porcelain so hard, that there's just no way that you were able to sleep through that. I return to the room and see your stupid face, that *stupid* face, just laying there, dreaming, about god knows what and who even cares anyway? I grab a cigarette and head to the deck where I gaze at the stars and think about how I got here, how I love every second of the journey and how it almost brings me to tears to be in a town where I can look to the sky and see the constellations, instead of that muggy mist. That orange sky filled with smoke elevated by police sirens that used to bring my mind to boil in another town long ago. The serenity and peace of the whole environment causes me to choke, and I can hardly swallow. As I toss the cigarette into the grass and head back inside, I blow a thick cloud of smoke through the door.

I try to go to bed, I really do, but I can't, and as you toss and turn I can't seem to find a good spot and I can't fall back asleep, and suddenly you ask me what's wrong and I say nothing and you ask me if it's Samantha, and I say "sure" and you start screaming at me and yelling at me all of a sudden in the middle of the fucking night mind you, straight up out of nowhere and I start to think that maybe you are just behaving irrationally through your sleep or because you're still drunk from earlier, but you're not, and you begin to get the best of me, firing all kinds of shots and all I can say is "babe, what the fuck?" but you can't calm yourself, and we're both sitting there naked just going back and forth when suddenly you reach for my knives in a panic since you know where it is I hide everything, and as you grab the big one I try to grab your hand to stop you, but I can't react fast enough, and you persist and push the knife deep into my gut and as I stare blankly into your eyes, I shed a tear stumbling, whispering, mumbling, "baby," and you just keep stuffing the blade with force into my stomach, and by now you're so caught up inserting it in and out and in and out, like a fuck about to cum, that I can hardly take it and you start laughing and giggling like a little kid demon, forcefully pushing me down to the floor, and weak due to blood loss, I fall so easily on the tile, feeling it cool against my back.

I can hardly move, and as I try to rise you put your foot on the knife still stuck inside my stomach and press it in deeper and deeper until it is lost inside me, and as I feel my ribcage crush due to the persistent steel, I can see you standing there, in the dark, looking as beautiful as ever knowing you won't get caught since you're such a fuckable item and no one would ever suspect your big blue gorgeous eyes, and it is then that you straddle me, cunt pushed up against my chin, squeezing my neck tight with your thighs like you're Sonya from Mortal Kombat with a sick finishing move in the third installment, and I must say although the wound has totally fucked me, I find this kind of arousing. *Why didn't you tell me you were into this sort of thing?*

But I can tell she's just lost it and even though I love her, I have to gain control before I bleed to death because if she doesn't kill me, the lack of medical attention sure as fuck will be sure to do so.

I push you off me but you quickly rise and now we're wrestling on the ground, and even though I have about a hundred pound handicap over you, I am losing so much blood and feel as if I'm about to faint, that you quickly gain control of the situation. I see you tilt your head to the right and give me this toothy grin you're so fucking famous for, as if to mock me, and I wonder what this is all about and begin to think about Spring Break when Samantha and I were going at it pretty hard even though I knew you knew, and now that she was gone and you were prone to weakness, we got back together and now I can see, as I piece it all together, that it was all just a part of your vengeance scheme and a plan to destroy my well being. *Don't you know this will fuck you in the long run? Don't you even care?* But you don't, in fact you can't even hear reasoning and strangely enough you begin to kiss me, heavily, deeply, passionately, and as I'm dying beneath you, I manage to fall in love with you all over again, and I regret ever having fucked that stupid bitch, and even though I was a weak one for blondes and you were a legit brunette with ab-fab tits, I couldn't avoid the temptation of the balder patch/greener grass ratio. *Come on baby, please forgive me…*

But it's too late.

You rise to straddle me once again, as I lay face up on the floor asking you "why, baby why?" as I continue coughing up blood, but you're deaf to reason and mute to explanation and you're in this killing-time-is-now-mode and I can't stop you, and I've totally lost this one, *the underdog is ahead by forty points at the half…* and I realize that you're just not going to stop until the job is finished and over, and I am said and done and dead and gone.

You grab my pocketknife and carve a giant cross in my face top to bottom left to right, big enough to crucify Jesus on and these aren't bullshit wounds, because I can feel the cool blood rush down my face in heavy gushes. You continue carving like an artist with a chisel, tongue stuck out to the right of your tight-lip shut mouth, and I can feel the fan pushing air against my torn skin flapping on my cheeks. I can tell my face is sagging due to the weight of the gash of the wound and by this point, it's really no surprise. I'm going to fucking die here and right before I black out in distant agony, I blow you a kiss with pouting lips and make sure you know that I always truly loved you.

European Postcard

You're not in any of them and I laugh. I laugh and I laugh until I am so gone and my face is prune purple and a giant vain is produced on my forehead from the pressure the skull is putting towards my smooth skin. By now I am so far away from where I was initially, that only a cool puff will bring me to my calm collected cool. You were never there and I had it all to myself. That was my goal; to distance you and to forget you. But regardless, it was Pam and I that were on the boat last March, and I can't forget how beautiful she looked before the abortion where she got that little pouch right below her belly button and I started losing interest, and no matter how many crunches and sit ups she did, it never seemed to go away. Samantha and I hadn't really sealed the deal yet and Tara hadn't even moved in and we were all so young still and god, how good was that giant buffet on the boat that afternoon, really?

Pam hits my arm with her elbow and tells me to quiet my breathing down as I can tell it's starting to get heavy. We're watching the new Ben Stiller movie, which is ok, but who am I to criticize since I'm not much of a fan anyways, and I thought *There's Something About Mary* was a total fag flick. I stuff my face with popcorn, eating it as if it's dinner, knowing full well I probably won't be eating again as I try to get closer to Pam, who is so caught up in the movie that she can't escape it and reality is nonexistent and so far away, that there is just no getting her back until the movie is over. I get up and go to the bathroom where I jerk off a quick one to a picture of her and her sister at homecoming that she has framed by the sink, and wash off neatly before returning. When I get back to the couch, Pam hasn't moved an inch. I check my phone to see the time since my watch broke a few days ago. Apparently, I got really drunk at Pratt's

Pourhouse the other night and started punching the wall before I got kicked out again. Doing so apparently broke the glass frame of my Fossil and it just shattered everywhere, and when I went out surfing up the north coast last weekend the salt water got into it and froze the dials and fucked it all up. So I didn't really even know what time it was.

I feel a new text message vibrate in my pocket.

It's from Sam, and she's got the drunk diction.

Wht Ru UP 2?

Nothing

Ahm at th Porhose

Great

m wt

?

I'm wet

This last line is enough to cause a stir and I tell Pam I've got to jet since I have class early tomorrow. Since she's such a zombie, she hardly hears my comments and barely moves as I rise to leave with no response. I reach in to kiss her but she just pushes me aside since I am in the way of the tv and before you know it I'm out the door, slick as a snake, in my car blasting Terror's latest on the way to the pub with no goodbye kiss. I'm looking good and feeling good and there is absolutely no stopping this and I've got a date with the devil, but as long as the devil is blonde, that is all that really matters.

When I get to Pratt's, I spy Sam sitting at the bar, surprisingly by herself. It's still early and the special is still going strong so I order a double pitcher and drink it to the bottom and before you know it I've had six which is equal to eighteen drinks according to DUI class math and I'm just trashed beyond repair and she's starting to sober up but she's loving that I'm out and when I play pool with the locals she massages my cock through my pocket and I win the game and before you know it we're out the door into the night and back at my place. Val phones and tells me he's got something he wants me to check out and since I'm down to party anyways, I tell him to head over and bring a few beers with him since I'm way beyond sauced and there's nothing worse to fuck your buzz than a Sober Joe.

When Val shows up, Sam and I have gotten so fucked up that we hardly pay any attention to the fucker but he cuts us a few lines on the counter and we're all up again, running around the kitchen when Sam suddenly tosses out the idea of a threesome and I must say even though I find the concept of Val a fucking mess, I declare to pick a hole and get to it. I must say double dipping with this fucker, no matter how rotted out, was always something to watch out for. Never rub the chicks your buddy has, since you know how sick you are, and there is a good chance those you surround yourself with are struggling with things that are much worse and often unidentified. Who knows what he's got?

I'm so caught up in it that I miss Pam's fourteen calls and three texts that go from "where'd you go?" to "What's up?" to "?" and before you know it, she shows up and she's at the door and the whole thing is fucked and I am totally caught, and at this point it doesn't even matter and I stand there naked in the living room, cock in Sam, with this disgusting buddy of mine with his dick in her mouth at the other end, just looking like a human clothesline, and as Pam is mentally digesting what's going on she quivers with big, white eyes that so tenderly begin to tear, and I can tell this image is just completely foreign to her, and I'm still here with Sam's hair held tightly around my grip, pulling it from behind her, and I must say the deceit makes me harder, and the fact that I'm caught drives me to burst inside Sam who I hope is on the pill, all while Pam still stands there.

But nonetheless, this was all so long ago that you've managed to get over it by now, and essentially this would all be behind us since we both know that your past is way worse than mine, and all the mistakes you've made when you were fucked, and all the bullshit that spewed out of that mouth while you've been sauced doesn't even compare to my interactions with others when I'm out. And I bet you're thinking, she must be pretty awful to top the drugs and the double fuck, and I promise you, we will get into that. She was rotten.

At Work

So Guest of Honor has decided to quiet up a notch and play this game even though I hold the upper hand, and he's been bleeding so profusely that when I come back from smoking a cigarette, he's quiet enough to allow me to think about how negative the nature of the whole thing actually is and just how unhealthy it is to creatively describe this scenario and how violent the nature of this prose has become. But I continue despite how sick to my stomach the confession makes me feel, since this is what I do and there isn't much to lose at this point. I dismiss just how damaging this whole thing is to me, you, or anyone else who's reading this, and I return to ash the cigarette and finish it off on Guest of Honor. Pam has already blacked out from shock and I sigh at the sight of this, but in reality, this is all so fucked that I have to walk away and stop since I don't like the feeling of the guilt since there is no one else here for me to talk to. Again, regardless of how this makes me feel, I have to finish these two and I have to finish the job I started. For some reason, the blue skies I used to think of in detail are so distant now, that it's almost impossible for me to conceptualize even one positive image.

Untying Guest of Honor and throwing him on the floor in furious anger, I am thinking about all the times he was hiding in my closet watching me toss my love, who is so peacefully resting, tied up to our right. I begin to tear his clothes off, why, I'm not sure, but am now stripping him to the bone. I take the darts we have by the board and begin shooting them at him, comically, yet with precise aim, as if every inch of his body is the bulls and he can barely rise sensing his defeat to the beefy local. I decide to finally end this ordeal since I just can't stand myself treating Pam like this anymore, but as I go to grab her off the ground she is just a rock. Still concrete. I touch her throat with two fingers checking her pulse for good faith, but there is nothing there. *There is just nothing there…* She rests so peacefully with my socks in her mouth and it appears that her face has swelled a bit since it seems as if she somehow has gagged on her own spit, and what I thought was silence turned out to be actually death.

I have Pam's dead body to deal with and I know there are supposed to be emotions involved here. Doesn't someone inside me even care? *Idle and thoughtless…* Idle and thoughtless, I begin to skin Guest of Honor with the machete, taking out all my anger on the fact that I am completely to blame for this whole mess and that no one else is responsible for this disaster. He squeals like a pig that's getting butchered for a roast, and there is just so much red going everywhere, blood on this, blood on that, on my face, and on my hands, on the floor, and just simply blood fucking everywhere, but I must end this now as I know Tara is going to be home soon, and to be honest, I don't think anyone is watching for her cat.

After all his muscles are exposed, I get on my knees and begin to tear away at his tendons with my teeth. I begin to chew heavily and deeply into him, and at this point I can't even sense his response. Due to the loss of blood he must have died a few minutes ago while I was so busy gnawing *feeling a craving, a need, a desire for the taste of human blood,* when suddenly, I just freeze. My actions create a stir so large inside my body that I'm caught in a loss that grabs hold of my every move, and it's then that I just stand there, solid still with a need that forces me to simply pause.

THE BEAUTY

I remember a couple years ago the whole family went on this great road trip. It started out as a damn mess with my sister and I shoved in the backseat of a Civic, but it turned into a real treat by the time the whole thing was over. We went to the Grand Canyon, where we got pictures of us riding donkeys all the way to the bottom, which at the time felt like a big waste of effort, but now that I think about it, turned out to be a rather special memory. We drove all the way to California where we took pictures of the Hollywood sign and managed to make it to San Diego to catch the Chargers game on Sunday since Dad was such a big fan. I guess it was his plan to make it to the game all along.

We left Phoenix a few days before and it was all Dad's idea anyway. It was Thanksgiving weekend and how he managed to get tickets for the game was completely beyond me. For some reason, Detroit still played every year, even though they always got their bags tossed and I know Dad didn't want to spend the day watching a rancid football game. This year they were 0-11 up against the undefeated Titans who were going to absolutely pummel them into the ground. I didn't mind missing the games since Dad was telling us he had a big surprise for Sunday. I knew what the deal was and acted surprised when he told us. Besides, the fact that he managed to lure Mom into going on one of her favorite holidays was a certain feat worth mentioning. She always did love to cook on the holidays.

This is the kind of exposure that makes me feel good, that I don't mind telling.

I don't need to get up in the middle of this story to smoke a cigarette. I don't need to go start the laundry to get my mind off the narrative. I don't need to distance myself from the illusory that makes me start to tremble and want to hold the family pet. This is the kind of stuff innocent youth is made of and even though I had already gotten laid when we went on this trip, I was still forever young and independent of my past mistakes.

San Diego got trashed by Atlanta, and even though Dad's team had lost, the camaraderie of the home game was a total blast. I would think about this trip years later as I got older and went off to college and caught every home game (even quitting a few jobs for the time off) and remembering how ridiculous those weekends were and how we would stay up all night, drinking throughout the day, and how much fun in the sun we had, and all the bars under the stars and how great it was playing around with everyone, wearing our colors with our faces painted, flasks in all our pockets. This is the glitter that identifies our lives. All the negativity deciphered and explored, and all the emotions that keep us up at night are meaningless. It is due to the lack of freedom and inability to live aside an over abundance of experience that haunts us in our dreams. Once we have been around long enough to know what's out there and that we are either missing it or fucking it all up, thoughts begin to dwell and leak into the everyday causing an inability to truly live, endure, and enjoy ourselves. It gets tougher and tougher as we get further down the line and mature in our years, and the lists, well shit, they have a tendency to get a whole lot longer as we get older, and the bills get higher and the stakes get harder, but it is our ability to understand our past and envision our future that makes us strive for perfection and desire the want and need for affection, love, and respect from others. We want to make those around us proud, we want them to look at us and say, "that's what I should've done." We want them to congratulate us on a job well done. We practically demand the recognition; from our friends, our family, and from those we love the most. We expect some sort of attention. We borderline demand it before we go into depression. But these virtues are not easily obtained and not everyone has similar standards. We must work hard to build the life we want to live and strive to make the most out of our existence. Never be crystallized in a lucid environment, never think it is so easy to express and feel. It is tough to get the point out there and never let being too wordy become your enemy. Ramble, let your thoughts roll, express yourself freely. Learn to understand and be compassionate towards others. Time makes you tougher and cold to the world around you. Do not let this haunt you. You can overcome the things that have brought you down. You can breathe easier once you let things go. Do not let time and pain impact your younger years as you will never get them back. You are always that kid you were in the backseat when you and your siblings were going back and forth and Dad had to backhand someone's face to get the car in order.

I don't care where I go when I die. These seconds count. Never distance yourself to forget, instead use the lessons from your past efforts and learn how to live.

Boys

Chuck has me coming over and frankly, I don't really care much for him anymore. That is, not as much as I do for Johnny anyway, who has a way bigger dick than Chuck does hard when he's just plain soft, *shah*. He was asking me how I feel about that real creepo Carl who hangs out around the house when his roommate's gone. I don't really mind it much, I mean, you hang with creeps for long enough you tend to lack a tendency to differentiate, *kah*. I guess you could say I *used* to love him. For like a minute, *shah*. It started out about two summers ago when we first hooked up. We met at this restaurant we both worked at, he was bartending and I was serving lunches. It was a decent lay. I remember we were both working the double one day, and we left our break to go smoke and fuck back at his place. It was decent. Needless to say, Carl was there. And as one thing led to another, it was a couple years and before you know it, I got used to it, he got used to it, and the whole thing just sort of spiraled from there. I didn't think much of it then, but I knew he just absolutely adored me. The sex was, *shah*, ok, and the consistency was something to speak for, but the monotony of his attitude and the way he just hated everything, I mean, it was such a complete turn off. I mean the guy was a total lunatic, *sooo* full of himself. He would go on rants, as if on a soapbox mind you, and just go off on topics like the total icon. He even went into his room once to construct an essay and came back out three hours later with the whole thing cited and fucking loaded with a complete biblio just to prove a point. He was the complete opposite of anything I ever was or could ever care to be with again in the future. It was great waking up back at his place when we were still going to school, *shah*. The schedules were nice. He lived so close to my classes I could just wake up and stroll down the street into the sidewalk and down the slippery slope of college ave. So yeah, that was always a perk.

But Johnny... Now there was something to get excited about. I loved it when we first met and he brought me back to his house to snort, just the two of us, and he was showing me all his shit and he was just so damn good at everything, and he was getting *sooo* into me being there, it was just absolute good solid shit. He lived by himself, so we did whatever whenever, and by three am I was butt naked on the flat top getting completely drilled while this Hawarya album he was so excited about was blasting in the living room, all the fucking lights on and the door unlocked, for sure, *shah*. *That was a boy who just knew how to get to work.* We fell asleep on the couch and only when Chuck called the next day, did I realize that it was four pm and the whole afternoon was gone and he hadn't heard from me since the night before, and I even had the audacity to tell him I was going to be staying in. Maybe the cheat felt hot and it could be the reason I got off on the whole idea of Johnny. Plus his name... Just saying his name got me going wet. *Johnny...*

But I guess that's why I still hang around Chuck. He doesn't give much shit about anything. I showed up the other day from the pool in that real tight pink bikini he picked up for me on v-day with three other guys I met earlier who got me completely trashed on codeine and all the beer I could drink and then talked about nailing me three way back at their apartment (which was so conveniently next door and up the stairs) but I respectfully said "no, I have a boyfriend," as I continued to giggle flirtatiously as I had been doing all day. He ended up offering them beers and got real excited about the company. I stayed late and sure, we fucked later that night, but that was when he asked me how I felt bout Carl and I said "I don't know Chuck, I really don't think much of him," and the next day I woke up and he wasn't laying next to me, and for some reason I felt worried.

But, like, *shah*, it was Thursday.

GREY OUTSIDE

The weather is a still and calm collected cool. Nobody inside is awake yet and the whole neighborhood took the trash out the night before aware of the cold the morning brings. It is freezing. Never mind the collected cool. The branches of the trees begin to crack and the mist from the gutters is rising to meet the wind that sways soothingly from left to right, and all that's heard is the beeping of a garbage truck nearby and the sounds of a car driving by from up the road.

Samantha looks ahead into the street, driving her coupe, thinking deeply about her next move. Only she isn't, it's just that her concentration on her thoughts confuses her and her face grins in a curious strain. Her stereo is blaring the latest Jamie's Elsewhere, which was only recently released, showcasing the stunning effort. She doesn't really dig it much. *Something about that voice...* Chuck had given her his copy of it last week when they both drove back up from Orlando rocking it out and yeah, they got a bit toppled off the shit he got from his roommate, and got totally baked in the back of Gregg's car when everybody was still inside watching the Bears destroy New Orleans in OT, but she regrets it, and this morning, it's all she's about and she's hoping that Pam is going to be at her place when she gets there, or else she's going to be Super Turbo Pissed II that she drove all the way out to Mandarin just to turn right back around with all this shit on her mind.

She pulls up to her house and sighs with relief seeing Pam's Civic on the lawn. The two had been friends since their freshman year in college and had hit it off from the start. They had both graduated from the same high school, but it was only when they moved into a different city, alone and afar from the comforts of a collected and familiar social community, that they established a bond and molded into complete duplicates of each other, the first complementing the second.

"Wake the fuck up, you slut!!" banging on the door like a cunt.

Samantha hears bottles rattling in the living room and can see Pam through the window, on the couch fully dressed and struggling to rise, her feet on the floor, as if attempting to sit up and great the visitor.

"What time is it?" asks Beloved Host as she rubs her eyes with the backs of her hands after she opens the door. She is so trashed she is not even noticing the scratches caused by her deep probing, *rings and bracelets tearing skin…* "Honey, stop it, you're freaking me out…" and Sam reaches to grab Pam's hands and put them down by her side. Pam looks like a total wreck but Samantha quickly spots a needle in the ashtray to her left, where a cigarette still sizzles and grabs it, furiously shaking the tool in Pam's face.

"What the fuck is this?! The cunt! As if I'm not one to worry about, you've topped the bottom!" Pam can hardly muster a reply. Samantha begins to think of all the guys they hang with in order to try and figure out where she got it from. It couldn't be Chuck, he was a total pothead. She knew the two of them had been fucking for years, which is why it was so great when she got in the middle and managed to mess it all up, needless to say it's what she did with everyone's guy. Samantha would be the best friend of a girl for say, a week, and then fuck her boyfriend the next just like the girls' pledge week. She *did* have the fake tits and a body that was so tight that you'd be a complete fag if you didn't throw yourself at the opportunity. Yet Pam didn't know they were fooling around behind her back yet. But for now, this wasn't the issue at hand. In this current shithouse of a situation, Pam couldn't tell you which nozzle hot water came from. Sam wanted Pam's phone for some answers and she reached into her pocket to grab it. Going down her cell, looking at numbers and missed calls, Sam was prying into Pam's personal life by going through her texts which seemed to go all the way up until fifteen minutes ago where she wrote

I thnk am Dyng

to Johnny T and Sam thinks, *that guy*. The total junkie coke fiend. He totally would be able to get the shit, but there's just no way he would have left Pam like this. At least, he would have stayed and fucked her. Wouldn't he? *Wouldn't you?* But this was total bullshit. Samantha calls Chuck on her cell, but gets no response and now she starts freaking out since she's worried about this cunt's hygiene habits and wondering how clean she is and if Chuck knows about this. After all, he *was* fucking her, was *he* clean? They hadn't used a condom in months, if ever for that matter, and the consistency on both parties was beginning to turn into a bit of concern for sweet, dear Samantha. A big dose of negligence from the two of them may have created a slight bit of a problem. For once, she had something to think about, as if this morning was not enough to ponder, and man, it was totally ugly, grey and cold outside.

Samantha feels a vibration on the couch and checks her phone and it's not hers and as she picks up Pam's cell she sees Johnny T calling, and Samantha answers it spitting into the receiver "what gives, asshole?" and he sounds really lost telling Sam to slow down, and he has no idea what's going on and tells her that Pam's text woke him up about ten minutes ago when his phone wouldn't stop shaking off the nightstand, only it doesn't sound like he's home at all. Shocked at Samantha's dilemma and afraid of any established misconceptions, Johnny tells her he'll be right over. But something about this whole mess just doesn't seem right to Samantha, and damn it, where the fuck was Chuck?

Devour The Dead

We were at Late Night when Pam was tugging my stuff, pulling down the sack out and in, telling me she wanted to go, and she was looking real good and I didn't really want to, but I was starting to worry about Chuck showing up, so I was like "fine, let's just get out of here," and before you know it, we were making out in the cab ride back home, and when we finally managed to get the door open and get into my house, I ran into my room and grabbed my iPod and blasted the new Mia's At Bentley's I just got that I couldn't simply get enough of. I personally wanted to stay out a little longer, but she wasn't going to stay up much later, not unless she got into some shit. We were just talking away when I whipped out the gear I got from Val earlier in the afternoon, and even though I wanted to go shoot up in the other room, I enjoyed hanging out with 'ol ass and tits watching her get all fucked up, a bit of a turn on, you can say. So she starts getting real chatty and asks me what I think of Sam and personally, I try to stay away from that one since she tends to cause quite a mess amongst everyone, especially those she isn't sleeping with, and even though I know that her and Pam have been great friends since our first year up here, I know she's fucked some of her closest friends and even though Pam and I give the tug just about every chance we get, there's no doubt that Chuck is rubbing Samantha at every opportunity that Pam and I are out at the scene together. That isn't to say that Pam isn't fed up with the guy, I mean it's only been a few months since she walked into his house when he wasn't answering any of her calls, that she caught him tag teaming Samantha with Val, slapping high fives, who is so indifferent to all this bullshit that it makes no difference that he was even there at all, really. It was only after I heard her coked up re-run of the whole story that I realized what a total fuck-off Chuck had been to her for years, and what a total fake Samantha was for pissing on her friendship like that with her so called "best friend." I was shocked at Pam's ability to completely forgive the cunt for betraying her in such a legitimate fashion. Needless to say, I wasn't anywhere near as innocent and this is all probably why she was sleeping with me in the first place.

So the night turns into morning and I decide I can't take it anymore, and when I go into the other room Pam follows me through, and when she asks me what I'm doing I tell her to fuck off but she opens the door and tells me in a bitchy tone "there is no way I am leaving without getting a shot," and only after she begs me for the better part of fifteen minutes and I refuse unconvincingly to let her try it, do I give up the debate and treat her right, and it's only seconds before the chemical surge takes hold that she gets so wet and grabs my cock, needle still in her arm, and starts stroking me so hard that I have to grab her wrist to indicate her need to ease up before she tears the fucking gear off. After we fuck she tells me it was just the greatest ever and then wants me to take her home. It's only then that I notice that she hasn't taken her shades off since we got to the house at one. She quivers in the passenger seat, laying on her side on the ride back to her house. When it gets time for her to get out and go, she looks at me and invites me in telling me she needs more. I didn't make much of it then and I may have still been drunk, but knowing then what I know now would have changed the entire scenario completely. Regardless, I give her what's left of the bag, which is the better part of a rather decent shot. She squeezes it into her palm and leans in to kiss me on the cheek. I drive off and head to The Patio in hopes of getting a few beers in me, but not even ten minutes into the session, Samantha calls me, livid from

Pam's. Safe to say it all could've very well been my fault. I look at my phone and notice that I missed Pam's text and I can't make out what it says, and as I try to calm Sam down, whose tone indicates that something completely fucked has happened, I can tell it is going to be impossible. I tell her I'll be over in five and when I wave the server over frantically and give him a twenty for the two beers I managed to punch in, I storm out of the bar and leave before he even has enough time to return with my change.

Last Christmas

Whosever idea it was to meet at the restaurant first was a brutal genius. It was such a great idea to get some grub and pre-drink the Christmas party we were all so excited about. It was just that we got so trashed before we met up with everyone, and well, let's just say that everything was just absolutely bloody perfect. Pam was wearing her silver dress with her banging ass being ever so complemented by the attire, and her earrings were just absolutely gorgeous. Chuck was even dressed real proper in a black and white scrunched suit, hair slick as wax. Samantha had brought two guys that she met at the mall earlier, all dressed very sharp, and by the looks on their faces, they knew Pam. Samantha, of course, outdid everyone in attendance, and poor Johnny arrived dateless, staring at Sam's enormous rack protruding from her short midriff as she teased him all night. The seven of us binged on margaritas and only after nine chilled rounds of 1800 shots did we decide to make a move to Kantra, the metro bullshit club the party was being held at.

Once we get through the door, I waste no time and head straight to the bar not giving a toss about Pam or Chuck or Johnny or Sam or the two fucking stiffs she dragged in with her. I order whiskey doubles and only after seven does the bartender cut me off, and only when I belligerently scream in dispute does security come over, and it only takes two seconds after that for me to spit on his face and before you know it I'm being dragged outside and the cops are there and the whole party is ruined and everyone is staring and now everything is just plain garbage and all of them are still outside looking, prying, thinking that I'm such a total freak, and I just take off running. Running and running, until molten lava begins to spill from every pore and my heart is about to explode, beating a battery power fuel, and by then I have gotten so far from the party that I call Cheryl and ask her what she's doing, and she sounds so pleasant and excited about the fact that I called that she asks "where are you?" and I say "down under," and I can't believe how far I've come and as she asks me "where the fuck were you earlier, Val?" my phone is blowing up a million calls a second, and it's then that I just toss it out and into the dark, dark night, with the moon lighting only the woods and somehow she just arrives a few moments later to where I am. So enchanted by her stupor, I lose myself and forget to go hunt the phone down, and as I ease into her bed as we get to her apartment, we go at it pretty hard, and it's total love and when she kisses me I shiver, and before you know it we're holding each other. Suddenly there is a giant thud on the door. An enormous end of the world bang in the other room. Ben storms in through the front screaming "what the fuck!" and I systematically rise and tackle him to the ground in full glory and Cheryl is in her bed just screaming, screeching her gooey lungs out. We wrestle on the floor for a few moments and when I reach for my pants to produce my knife, Cheryl lets out an enormous "NO!" and as I carve deeply into Ben, sticking him ever so hard, not giving a fuck about him or his life or his stupid fucking face, just simply fed up with the presence of everyone tonight, I fade out into a deep blank and recognize my emptiness in this, as me and Cheryl may now actually be official.

WRAPPING UP

The dead. The two of them are dead. Tara is on her way home, the cat totally dipped, and the two of them are dead. This might shut up the social circle a little bit, or at least knock it back down to size. Everyone remembers what happened to Val last winter when he totally took Ben out when he caught him in the sack with Cheryl. The attorney managed to take it down to self-defense since Cheryl hated Ben anyway, and in fact, was glad he was gone. The whole thing was totally a horrid morbid. Her testimony was a complete lie and Val was looking at a minimum sentence due to her lack of morality. Sure, Ben had an awful drinking problem, but it's not like Val was born a saint. That night when Val totally slashed Ben apart, a new relationship developed between him and Cheryl. Val did about eleven months of his two-year sentence but since no *real* weapon was produced, and Val didn't *technically* kill Ben (it was actually just the three pints of lost blood in the ambulance), good conduct was enough to get Val back to us in the community just a few short months later. Cheryl completely loved Val and now that his actions had just about been branded on his forehead, Val became the total knock-off hard cunt to the rest of us. But as you very well know by now, or at least damn well better fucking should, it was only a matter of time before Sam was hanging around us again, and once Pam told Cheryl that him and I both got to her, everything was destined to go down the shitter. That night destroyed everything in every aspect, and even though Pam never minded or mentioned the event to me in the future and I had put it behind me, for some reason Cheryl was so fixated on her maniacal boyfriend that she was unable to let it go. Unable to forgive. I haven't heard the whole story, but from what was made clear to me, Cheryl was sleeping over at Val's the other night, and from what I could understand, Cheryl started arguing with him and getting into some real heavy shit about them and Samantha, and before you know it she stabbed him fourteen times; eight in the gut, six in the face and was looking to be in solitary confinement at this point awaiting her court date, and possibly a general population migration. But she at least had the cash.

My actions are in total accordance with my environment, and I take the shovel I found in the garage and dig two eight-foot holes in two random spots in the backyard. Needing to piss, I turn to Guest of Honor's corpse and display my cock and balls, cupping them just beneath, and unleash a mean fury of hot stinky pee that drains itself down his neck from his eyes and mouth, and even though I know I'm going to need to move him later, I'll just use the pair of latex gloves in the kitchen that will make sure I don't get my hands covered in urine. At this point I am just so absolutely smothered in blood and tendons and assorted bits and pieces of skin and bone and this and that, that it doesn't really matter anymore. *The job is dirty, and dirty deeds get done.* I remove the two bodies and put them in one of the two holes respectively, then cover them in dirt. I don't make much of Guest of Honor, but there's just something in me that breaks when I toss Pam's body into the hole and begin to cover her face, that sweet fucking face, my face, with dirt, and there's just something not right about this whole thing, and everything is so fucked and no no *no* it wasn't supposed to be this way, and what the fuck am I going to do now... Even though I'd been seeing Sam on and off for the latest, it didn't matter because right here right now, I love Pam and need her and want her to come back and say *I'm just kidding! Look! I'm Alive! See? It's alright!* like she always did, being the joker that she was, and before I can even catch myself, I hear Pam's phone ring in the garage, and when I go check out who it is, I accidently hit answer and I can hear the guy on the other end "Hello? Hello?! Pam?" but I just freeze. After a few seconds it hangs up. But then it rings again and again and again and all throughout the night for that matter, and I notice that the missed calls are from Johnny and I wonder, what the fuck he could possibly be doing calling her up this late, and since when were they talking? And what am I going to do when everyone is wondering just where Pam had run off to, asking me if I knew where she was?

BLUE INSIDE

Samantha calms herself and goes into the living room and turns the tv on and waits for Pam to get out of the shower. Just what could have possibly gotten into her? Was she being torn apart from within that she just had to find a means of escape? It was Samantha's job to juggle the cocks of her social life, and maybe Pam just wasn't cut out for it. Samantha hears a knock on the door and before she can even get up to open it, Johnny comes in through the room, an evident case of the completely wasted, and whether it's from the night before or from this morning, doesn't really matter much to her and she begins to attack him, hitting him in the chest with her palms in such a furious fashion that Johnny has to grab Sam by the wrists and struggle with her all the way down to the couch just to get her to stop.

"Can you tell me what this shit is all about?! I know you had something to do with this!" Johnny stares at Sam's beet red face as it swells in anger. Why did Sam care so much for her friend's well being? Not everyone knew, but Sam was clearly going to town on ol' Chuck who was dating Pam for, I don't know, let's just say well over two years now. Even though Pam had caught them in the act when Val was still around, Pam never seemed to break it off with him. But why would the friend Sam so leisurely betrayed be of any importance to her at all? This was the twisted nature of our dear social group and even though everyone hated each other and talked the trash behind everyone's back and laughed at everyone's shortcomings, they would still all get drunk together and fuck together and it was safe to say that pretty much all their faults and failures could be blamed on each other and were essentially measured by those around them. Johnny's lack of an explanation for Sam sends her over the edge, but as soon as she threatens to call the cops Johnny strikes her in the face, and tells her to cool it. She is so shocked by his actions that she can hardly move and she can tell that it's already begun to swell and that it's going to seriously bruise and that this hit will leave a mark. Deep down inside, Sam knows how he feels about her and how she's whoring herself out to Chuck, and Johnny T can't stand the sight of this cunt, and even though he cares for Pam, he doesn't want to see her hang around with the likes of this one even though he's the one she needs to be worried about in the first place. Besides, who was he to speak? Wasn't he too being an unfaithful resident of their current epoch?

"I'm going to stay here and clean this place up, and you're going to leave and not worry about what you saw here today." At this Sam becomes furious, and refuses to cooperate until her friend is in good hands. "I'm not just going away John!" He takes a deep breath, and turns over to her and sighs "look, I'm the one who got her into this mess, and now that I think of it, I shouldn't have left her unattended, and I don't know what I was thinking. Fine. But I'm telling you, we don't want to make a bigger deal out of this than we should and get everyone else involved. *Fucking* trust me. We are done talking about this." Sam is at a loss and goes into the bathroom and locks the door.

She comes out a few minutes later and kneels next to Pam. "Are you going to be okay? Johnny's here, he says he's going to stay for a while." Sam is sickened to her stomach and tells Johnny not to try anything funny, but he's sitting motionless in the loveseat with his shades on not saying anything at all. As Sam gets into her car and leaves the driveway, a bit confused about everything that just happened, she sees that she missed Chuck's call while she was inside. With Johnny over at Pam's, she takes advantage of the opportunity and heads over to his place for the juicy details.

DETAILS

"Sorry I missed your call, what's up babe?"

The tone in Chuck's voice is enough to drive Samantha to the wall, but so far her whole day has been a complete toss up, and she's so pissed that Chuck didn't answer when she called him earlier this morning that she just blurts out her frustrated rambling.

"Your girlfriend is a total fucking junkie mess, do you know that? I found a syringe in her ashtray Chuck. A syringe!" Chuck is silent for a few seconds as if trying to digest the information, and Sam awaits a response, but he makes no reply to this alien comment.

Chuck had no idea what his girlfriend did when he wasn't around. He had heard from his friends about the way she presented herself in public, and the way she would get so fucked up and stumble back home into his bed. He didn't mind it as she was a decent ride, and besides she would *always* end up in his bed. Last Saturday, he had heard the story from Sam when the two of them had gone out to CJ's sports bar for ladies night. Apparently, Pam had gotten so trashed that when she squatted to piss outside in the parking lot between cars, her heel tilted and she slipped, blacked out with her panties down to her knees with her pussy out, and fell asleep momentarily on the gravel. When they would go out together it was one thing since they would just get sloppy sauced and find a stall to fuck in and hit up Cathy's Wings And Subs on the way back home, sharing a chicken finger basket with plenty of bread and butter, before getting rough back at the apartment. But by the sound of it, Charles had no idea his Betty was on the silly shit. To him, Sam was such a total wank-off that when she called him he didn't mind if his mother was ill, or if his dad had died, he had cum on the brain and was ready to shoot it between her teeth and those wonderful, heavenly majestic pair of tits. "Why don't you come over and we'll talk about it? I'm kind of busy right now." She's a bit caught off by his response. *Okay...*

"Why didn't you answer when I called you?"

"Babe, its 12:30, just what do you want me to do?"

On her way over, Sam smokes about four menthols and wonders why she's still in town, since she doesn't even go to school anymore. When Cheryl went ape shit and we lost Val, and by now Ben was a distant memory, Sam could hardly concentrate on anything besides her senseless paranoia in her weak pathetic drama clique for the better part of a good six months. Now, Chuck was able to get some of that trash off her mind, since he hardly noticed what he ate for dinner, let alone what his girlfriend was doing, or what Sam was doing for that matter. Since he always had plenty of pot it was always a pretty chill place to stay. After all, Samantha never really minded his company, and besides, he was a decent lay.

When she gets over to his place, Chuck already has the bong packed, watching the Florida State game on tv and even though they're 7-3 this season, it doesn't look like they'll be heading to the conference championship, and they should be lucky enough to even land a bowl, and before you know it, Chuck has his tongue down Sam's throat and she's going for his cock, and he's unbuttoning her pants, and when he goes for her bra and realizes she isn't wearing one, he just rips off her shirt, and two minutes later she's laying on the couch ass up, with Chuck towering over the back of her head, looking to move towards a position to tittie fuck, and god, she thinks, it's these situations that make me feel so motherfucking ugly inside.

GAMEDAY

After an hour and a half of sitting in the living room watching football on this little trashy, beat up dvd/tv combo waiting for Pam to come out of the shower, she finally gathers her shit and sits next to me on the couch, wearing nothing but her baby doll Emmure shirt, a leopard thong (extra-small, thank you), and her D&G shades which complement her black streaks in a stunning fashion. Even though what I think we're dealing with here is a bad comedown or an awful hit, I thank her for not overdosing, and when I think about it, there's just *no way* she could've since what I left her with was barely anything at all. Certainly not enough to be bothered by, and just the fact that this has been blown out of proportion like this, brings me back to last night when we were at Late Night and how she was playing with my cock, and when we got back home all we did was talk. Now that I think of it, I still haven't busted my load and it's been, like, well over six days now. I order us sandwich delivery since it looks like she could use the protein, and even though she hardly touches her wrap when the food arrives, I stuff my face full with a turkey and roast beef delight with plenty of provolone and about half a gallon's worth of oil. By now the games are over until the next one at eight, so I tell her to get dressed so we can go out for the nightly drinks and burn the whole day off. As she runs to her room, there's just something I notice about the way that ass shakes, and as I follow her in and grab her arm while she's searching through her closet, I turn her around and begin to kiss her hard, thinking, knowing full well that Chuck is with Samantha right now and that I am with his girlfriend, who I've been with all night, getting her fucked up on all sorts of shit, and as I rip off the thong that's been teasing me all day, I reveal a tight pink little box, and as I pounce right on top of her and begin to pound in and out, in and out, still wearing everything but my pants, I hear a slight whimper. I look at Pam and see that her eyes are closed and little tears are starting to come down her face, and at this point I don't know if it has something to do with me, or Charles, or the fact that she just shot up heroin for the first time, and she says "no, you're just so fucking big, I feel like it's ripping apart my insides." So this is nothing to be worried about, and we keep going as she just needs to learn how to take it as they all have in the past.

The girls in this town have definitely taken a direct hit in regards to quality and professionalism. They're all sleeping with everyone, so all the guys are cool since everyone's getting laid, but aside from that, all they do is piss and moan and get bitchy about everything. If it's not the drugs, it's the party, if it's not the party, it's the outfit, if it's not the outfit, it's the sex, if it's not the sex, it's the size of the dick, and if not that, then they all cry about how fucked up they got the night before and tell tales of complete and utter garbage, and I swear these are all walking vaginas, full of disease, toxins, and contamination and if they didn't have tits they would all be walking with bounties on their fucking heads. None of us here even care, and nobody is doing anything about it, but since the girls look so good, and the nights get so hot, who really cares how good Florida State is doing this season?

Pam and I go out to The Patio where we drink margaritas for a few hours and watch the Trojans bury UCLA. It's then that she fills my head with all this useless bullshit about Samantha and how she has hpv, and Chuck and how he's fucked her even though he knew, and as she starts getting more and more comfortable and slightly more impacted by the drink, she mentions that cruise she never went on that Chuck totally fucked her out of, something about an abortion last summer, Samantha's boob job and its symmetry, her workout routine and how it's totally gone to hell, Chuck's roommate Carl who is a total pervert apparently, and how she doesn't really give a shit about what happens after graduation since everything has already fallen apart anyway.

At the end of the night we go back to her place, and surprisingly Chuck hasn't called all day. When we watch Sportscenter back at her place on that little shitty tv she's got, replaying all of the games we just watched, she works up some pot she managed to get from her roommate who never seems to be over when anyone else is, and even though I have never met the guy, I still think its super turbo cool that we have something to smoke at the end of another awful and depressing Saturday in our poor excuse for a winter season. As the top 10 begin to roll off the screen, I can see Pam has already blacked out, and as I smoke the rest of the bowl my eyes can hardly stay open, and the force it takes to fight sleep is beyond me, and next time I remember waking up, it's Monday afternoon.

II. Blonde Glow

BREAKING

The night is here again, and everyone is getting their faces on and I can hear all the girls laughing in the bathroom as they attempt to get their act together before we miss the special. I sit in the living room, peacefully nursing a beer, as Johnny comes in through the door and he looks, well, okay really, nothing special, blah… Even though we have the same jacket on, I paid more for mine and I look better in it dead than he ever will, and this tid-bit of knowledge makes me resent his acquaintance, and even though we somehow manage to get along in every sense of friendship when we go out with the girls, I still can't stand the guy and his needy nagging tendencies.

"We going to get fucked tonight, brah?!"

Right. Just the way he looks at me when he's asking this is so pathetic that I want to stretch his bottom jaw over his head and crush his teeth into the back of his skull through his forehead, and kick him down three flights of stairs with a knife in his back, performing the spine crunch specialty. I know five minutes into the bar he's already going to be bugging me to get him some more shit, even though I know he's failing all of his classes this semester and probably shouldn't be, and I know that everything has spiraled out of control for him. He's going steady with Pam who tends to roll with that trash Chuck, who's been giving the boot to their dirty friend Sam that I've been hearing so much about, I know the dish has got hpv and it's really nothing anyone should be eating out of, but everyone around here refuses to get tested and come to terms with the truth.

I finish my beer and leave Johnny in the living room by himself and go check in on the girls in the bathroom. Two of them aren't even fully dressed yet, one still in her underwear. Straight long hair, banging makeup applied seamlessly, lips pouting red. At this point I know we won't make it to the bar on time, and we'll surely miss the special, and damn it, I've only brought ten dollars. I'm so pissed that I go into the other room and punch the wall three times until I calm and then head back into the kitchen and search the fridge for the slightest bit of liquor, beer, sushi, *anything* at all that could bring some sort of connection with at least one my senses.

I spot a tiny party size bottle of whiskey in the pantry and calm my gestures as I find relief in the taste of alcohol. I bring the iPod from my car and plug it into the living room stereo revisiting past classics such as Burnt By The Sun's *Blowjob City*, a total gem off their Luddite Clone split, and *Nobody Takes Pictures Of The Drummer* off my Nora favorite but it's really only a matter of seconds before Angelica comes from the bathroom, completely surprised and caught off guard by Johnny's presence, and first of all, he wasn't invited? and tells me to turn off this "bullshit." I sigh, and blast *In Da Club* and as she frolics back into the bathroom in approval, I can hear the rest of the girls blow drying their hair and can even smell their CHI's heating up, thinking didn't they already do this step? As each of them begins burning handfuls of blonde and black, I wonder how the sockets in the bathroom haven't given in yet and torched the house to flames.

Johnny nods in confidence of Angelica's firm physique and looks to me for approval, and I just scoff and honestly, I've had enough of this cat. If it weren't for Pam, one of Angelica's younger sorority sisters who I don't think is even enrolled this semester but somehow manages to whore her way around campus and her rent and pretty much just life in general, I would probably never have to see this brown-eye again. My understanding of the whole thing is that Angelica met Pam during rush week and she had all the right connections to all the top notch shit for being such a young chick in a new town. Angelica embraced her aggressive younger pal and showed her the ropes of Greek culture and the rest pretty much snowballed from there. It wasn't even four weeks into last semester that they both took part in the College Invasion tour and blew about four guys in the "Booty Beach Babe Blowout" online feature, each alternating holes, with 416 Sigma Eta's viewing in attendance. I think Pam had a boyfriend somewhere around these parts, but we never saw the guy, and Johnny had always hung around since the first time I had ever even met Pam anyway. Although I had heard of a Chuck before, for some reason the only guy I ever saw was Johnny.

Angelica and Pam come out of the bathroom and Cindy joins us in the living room at last, indicating we are all ready to finally leave. I must say the wait was worth the effort, since all three of these chicks have the ass and tits that scream to god and he screams back, and after all the wait and anticipation, I finally realize that being seen in their company is worth the patience, and even though Angelica and I had been friends since high school and fucked on a pretty constant basis, I always enjoyed talking to the other girls more and luring them back to the apartment and sharing the dirty grope with her the next day. Besides, she had her own thing going on from what I would later figure out.

When we finally get to the bar, Cindy is just all over my cock, and in all honestly, I kind of like it. All the efforts I have to do to go out and hit on someone new or bullshit with another dumb girl about how her friends couldn't keep up with her at happy hour are useless. I am the gatekeeper, herding hungry pussy a la carte, leading it back to the house. I can tell Cindy is operating on a few anti-depressants, so I ease up my approach a bit as it's completely unnecessary to even work on this one. I still take advantage of the opportunity, and as we make our way across the dance floor and out onto the patio, we manage to make our way towards the women's bathroom, I can hardly contain my hard-on and it's a good thing we get to fucking quick, because it's only five minutes into the score that I shoot my muck deep inside her tubing, and as she sighs in relief I can feel her lips quiver on my dick, and as I wipe off the muck from beneath, and she puts her leg down from up on the toilet seat and wrapped around me, I pull up my trousers, and suddenly she's just laying there, already trashed, useless and distraught, with her bare ass on the toilet. I help her rise, and after ten minutes of feeding Gerber to a two month old, we are ready to leave the stall.

When we get back inside, I can see Pam and Johnny are heavily making out on the dance floor and their faces part every few seconds to breathe. I can see their tongues wrap and roll within one another like serpents in hell, making my head spin that I have to fall back over to the bar for support. Cindy and I head to the girl who was getting us the really strong gins earlier, which is right beside where Angelica stands, who is talking to a few guys she met earlier at happy hour. By the looks of it, I think they're coming back to the apartment later. Pam and Johnny disappear and we don't see them for the rest of the night, and it's only a few minutes later that I tell Angelica I have to take Cindy home before she gets arrested. It's only a few minutes after that and I'm back at the apartment with Cindy and we're both sweating heavily tearing each other's clothes off, and the next day she can't remember a damn thing and when I call Angelica, she doesn't answer.

TIME

The other day I was over at Pam's apartment when she told me to sit and wait in the living room. I got so red and almost started to boil that I almost freaked, but she was out in just a few seconds, and I guess she was just talking to her Mom anyway, and once I calmed down a bit, I guess I was finally cool with it. I have noticed a bit of distance between the two of us, and even though I've been messing around with Samantha on a pretty consistent and frequent basis, and well, we've been pretty much romping like, well, all the time now, I still make time for Pam. Even though her friends have probably been getting the best of her and taking her out with them every night, we still manage to find time in between to get rowdy, even though Carl always manages to be at the house every time we take our clothes off.

I took her out to lunch, and not once did I manage to get a glance at her eyes since she never did take those hideous sunglasses off I got her last fourth of July at Solstice. When she told me about Angelica and Cindy (two girls which I've never met) and how they both got totally out of control on the pills the other night, I started spacing out and thinking about inflicting pain on Carl and how I wish I could create an iron maiden and strap him to it and fuck Pam out of her concrete mind right in front of him, even though knowing his creep tendencies, he would probably get off on that sort of thing. I pay the check and Pam gives me complimentary road head back to the house.

As I zone out and look into the distance of the road, I cannot think of things getting any better, when Pam suddenly stops and removes her lips from my cock interrupted by a phone call and says a horny "sorry, baby," with spit running down her bottom lip.

Apparently Johnny T was calling her for reasons I don't know, and for one I didn't even know they were friends. But I guess it's all my fault since I've been spacing out a bunch lately and paying more attention to Samantha, that I really hadn't noticed what she's been doing and at times don't even remember how many days go by without us even seeing each other.

I drop her off at her apartment and kiss her lightly on the lips, and for a quick second I fall back in love with her, truly, madly, deeply, like that fag-disco jam Savage Garden released when I was younger with the cherry cola. I call Sam on the way back home and ask her what's up and she asks if I'm down to chill later, but since Pam just blew my load to another planet and I'm full from lunch, I tell her I'm a little too tired to roll and when I go home I stuff a blunt so thick and plan my vicious attack diligently.

LUNCH

Angelica and Cindy go to Mika's for lunch where they both get veggie turbo's. Even though Cindy doesn't really like hers that much, she picks at it with a fork and when Angelica is finally finished eating, they get into Cindy's pink H3 and listen to the new Barley The Rat on their way to the mall. "So you and Neal totally fucked the other night…" Angelica urges persistently, like a total nag, but still smiling nonetheless. *The other night,* Cindy thought. Everyone had gone their separate ways, which Angie thought was totally fucked and the fact that her two friends left her behind with the guys she met earlier in the day was totally twisted as they could've been total creeps and treated her rough. Fortunately for her they weren't, and they didn't get ugly with her, and even though Angie resented her friends for leaving her, she was glad to have the apartment to herself when Daryl and Biff came back to her place later, and she got to experience double anal for the first time, even though she never did hear the end of it from Paul.

"Whatever, it's not a big deal or anything, it's not like you've never fucked him… Like, you *sooo* can't be mad at me." Cindy was aware that Angie and Neal had been friends for-e-ver. Even though they fucked on a pretty regular basis, they never really made much out of it and for some reason, none of their friends ever said more than two words about the issue. However, Cindy was feeling guilty about sleeping with her roommate's fuck buddy and could understand her friend's concern, which in this case was almost disguised as resentment.

"Look, Neal and I are best friends. Pretty much have been our whole lives. What he decides to do is his own prerogative and

I'm sure he feels the same about me. As far as you're concerned young lady, I think you need to put your priorities in order because next time you leave me alone like that you'll wake up with the face full." Cindy didn't really mind her friend's aggressive demeanor towards her, but she knew just how ugly she could get. She didn't really want to mess with or even test Angelica's violent ambition and felt a distance growing between them. Although Angie was just kidding with her good friend, Cindy had seen the way she handled the younger sisters. She was there when Angie wore their underwear for a whole week on her period with no tampon in sight. She was there when she got drunk and rubbed their brushes in her cat's litter box. She saw Angie steal cash from the pledge's bags during initiation week and how she spread vicious rumors about them during socials. Pam, Angie's *little sis,* had to convince the entire fall '04 of Alpha Sig's that she didn't have hpv, and only until she actually went to the health center to get a physical and an annual pap smear and displayed the results all over the chapter house on their monthly social, did Angie finally back down and apologize on behalf of Pam, and made a direct decision to announce her initiation into her family on Big-Little night. The two wouldn't hang out much throughout the years, but the bond had been recognized, if at *least* established for that matter. Cindy had met Angie years ago in school. They decided not to discuss their future plans with each other and see where they would go in their respective futures. They moved to the new town to get away from the local clique and instead of breaking away from one another, what they found was each other at opposite ends. With new crews, sure, but I mean, that was a pretty hardcore ballsy thing to do, eh? But these days, Cindy could hardly focus and felt awful inside. She felt far from what she was set out to establish and what she thought her soul was destined to do. These days, Cindy could hardly recognize her own reflection and felt worried that if something didn't happen soon, she wouldn't even be able to look at herself at all.

SHOPPING AT THE SNAKE

So I'm at the mall sipping on a latte when Chuck calls, and I have to literally put my bags down and place my drink on a table in order to reach my phone that's buried in the depths of my Louie. Chuck seems to be rambling, in fact I have no idea what he's getting at, really. Sometimes I wish he would just leave that slut Pam and I could just write her off and everything would be perfect, except that knowing me, I'll probably just string him along for a couple of weeks before he would get fed up with my trash and we would be over and he would go back for Pam, only she would be too busy getting sick with that Johnny T bum she's been hanging out with lately, that personally, I'm not too fond of.

Does he want me to come over? I really don't know why he even called. I hang up the phone and plan on heading towards the new Coach that just opened up that for this mall, is actually pretty impressive. I spot two totally hot guys, obviously shagable, blatantly checking me out from the Vizno smoothie booth. Although I could ask them what they're doing later and where they're going and in twenty minutes be back at an apartment getting drilled, I'm so conveniently on my period that just the thought of insertion makes me feel queasy and get chills that I suddenly feel like I'm going to throw up.

Looking at all the stores as I pass them by staring down the mannequins wondering what it'd be like to be one, thinking, dreaming, slipping into another world where I am free from all this trash, I exercise an approach towards steady breathing. I find myself spending thousands; buying purses, jackets, heels, slip-ons, slip-off's, candy, mascara, lip-gloss, coffee, a gift card for father's day, a card for Mom, and before I am even still enough to gain my heart rate back from just barfing up cash, I come to terms with everything, and establish an equilibrium.

I am such a whore and everybody knows.

I have yet to make an impact and I continue to dwell in this sea of wretched attitude. What fucking gives? I suddenly start getting really depressed. Frustrated, I walk into Cico's Coffee and get a small cup of joe and drink it black. For some reason, I quickly find myself making my way out of the mall and into my car and on the way over to Chuck's without even thinking about it. Suddenly, I realize that I never really ever even committed to leaving the plaza and now I happen to be driving.

FIVE SECONDS TURN INTO A WORLD OF PROBLEMS

So clearly by now, everything has already gone to hell, and this you already know. I cannot just bury her this way, *I just can't…*

I dig her body out of the ground and take her back into the garage.

Quickly, skillfully, smoothly… I will make this work. Give me a minute now. Give me a few seconds to think and I will sort this through. No need for theory of the stairwell here. No need to think about how I should've handled this whole thing. *Take your time, do this right.* I believe it was Palahniuk that once depicted the short story in which the man would be able to formulate a vindictive comeback return with a comment that will gain attention and the notoriety it deserves only after he has already left the party in which he was being ridiculed. I will pull them apart and scatter them. I will put them in different spots of the yard and that will sort this out. *Yes, that would be the case.* This sure is a damn mess, though. Feeling the guilty ill now, and that's for sure. But right now I need to start acting quick with skill as this is serious bloody business here. Tara is going to be coming back soon, and that cat. *That fucking cat.* I start to call for Darla attempting to get her home since after I am done with this nonsense I don't want to start searching the whole neighborhood for that filthy, disgusting thing. But I can't focus on one thing at a time for some reason. I start sawing methodically. I do Guest of Honor first. As if an appetizer, before slicing into a thick Pam steak tearing her into bits, ripping through her skin, pulling her form apart, just mangling her shape and gorgeous design. The air is a thick coat, and the bugs are buzzing in the trees. A mosquito sticks to the sweat on my arm. I can rest when this is finished. I will be able to rest then, yes.

But Pam... when this is finished...

My dear sweet Pam, baby, what will I do without you? What will I do with you gone? Sam was probably one of the least of my concerns even though we were hitting it off rather well and certainly on the regular. I wonder when I'd see her again. Just about the time before I black out from nausea at the ugly revelation of my actions and destructions of my one true love, I fall into thoughts of soothing mists and summer gusts of purple extreme breeze free falls that circle in endless rotation on a terrace floor, and then, in the height of callousness, I transform.

NIGHTS

So one of the local heavyweights happens to be releasing a new one next month, and I just find it *sooo* appropriate that they happen to be playing in town tonight, and for some reason I just think it's *sooo* necessary for Cindy to come with me even though I know she likes that aggro-poppy retro mix that's just *sooo* convenient and fashionable right now. Even though I don't think it's all that bad, I just simply don't respect her opinion when it comes to music or culture or news or anything at all for that matter, and think that everything she's into is just because her friends are into it, and everything from her shoes to her million different outfits just remind me of a chameleon molding into their environment whether it be a solid rock, a sunset, or a chemical formula, they simply manage to blend into anything as they're sizzling in the desert sun and I just blow in there and VROOOOM! come crashing down in full force all over it with my Grave Digger monster truck squishing its fucking insides, until they've become its outsides, painting whatever rock it happened to be resting on in whatever shade it managed to mold into. Well *anyway*, we're going to this show and I'm super turbo excited here and I throw my kicks on, turn off the tv and head over to Cindy's at full speed knowing that she'll probably still be sleeping when I get there, even though it's already like, 8pm. On the ride to her place, I almost drown myself in thoughts of graduating, leaving this town behind, Balooah, the singer's outrageously red hair, my saggy seat belt, traveling to the Philippines, steaks, sushi, a strange love for little dogs, Chuck's party, moving on, Pam, the future, that sunset, death, roller coasters, Walt Disney's I in his personal signature, Fred's bar-mitzvah, and that little Asian girl that came and sang me happy birthday when Eugene took me out to dinner last year at Zirgah-Li.

I bang a few times on the door after ringing the chime, and when she doesn't answer I just help myself in since the door was so conveniently unlocked. Cindy is still in bed as expected, laying on a queen size mattress that is overflowing with white linens and one hell of a thick duvet which I want to find myself blacking out all over in, dragging to it my filthy bourbon feet from the show. I plug my phone into an auxiliary chord that's laying around connected to her speakers and just blare *The Downfall Of Us All* at about thirty-two and it doesn't even take two seconds for the ol' breakdown to kick in and this girl just flies across the room which is perfect, since she likes to sleep naked. Not only do I manage to get a sick laugh out of the whole deal, but I also get to glance at the munch a quick bit and stare the minge, and although she hasn't shaved in a few days, I guess I can work around it.

"Are we going to this show tonight or what Cindy?"

"What *show* Neal? I don't know what the fuck is going on. What time is it?" she sighs as she wipes the crust off her eyes, rising from the floor.

"It's almost eight. You blacked out on the shit again. You're not going to remember tomorrow. You're not going to remember right now. So get up, you're coming with me, and you'll appreciate this." And now it changes. It's a wonderful thing with these street pills and how these women just get hooked on the conspiracy of the nightlife, Neal thought. So dangerous to the process, so tedious to produce, they don't ever find themselves too scared to come in contact with the wild. These little girls that become these machines that consume and destroy, consume and destroy. Over and over again, they seek to live, breathe, and with plans to decimate, they thrash and burn and even though it's all so dull, and oh so demanding, it makes the pleasures of the night go by. But be careful if you're caught in their presence, as you might be held responsible and often deemed accountable for the mess they create.

Cindy manages to throw on a real short jean skirt and a green tank top that just *absolutely* complements her figure, and although she just rolled over she looks like a million bucks and her eyes are so blue, her head is so blonde, and that face is so small in comparison to the rest of her body (which is all very much *sooo* in proportion) with her heavy mascara bordering beacons that are struggling to keep steady, that it almost makes Neal want to drool. As she asks him who is playing tonight, he goes into detail about how great their Rise debut was and what a big kick they all got out of it when it was released, and even though he wasn't really talking to the generic crew last summer, they still enjoyed the group together when they met at the shows. He keeps going on and on about how great their choreography on stage can be, and Cindy just keeps dozing in and out of consciousness, often almost inching towards banging her head on the dashboard a couple times. But it's alright, because he knows that the minute she gets inside she's going to start a tab and before you know, it will be last night all over again and he'll have to fight off three cocks before she's bathing in cum.

And it changes back. We get downtown and I park the car (Cindy fast asleep in the passenger). I go over to the other side and open up her door and she just slimes out of it like a snake in Eden. As I scrape her off the sidewalk wishing I had a spoon to scoop this soup with, I ask her if she wants to go back and she says "no, Neal, *no...*" and with that okay we're well on our way, and she's up and ready all of a sudden telling me how much she loves me and how much fun we have together and that she wishes she would've driven and how she's sorry that she fell asleep on the way over and for an instant, I almost believe her and I think of all things we could be: a future, kids, a dog, a house, a pool, Christmas, a swing in the backyard, but before I can even mutter a word of my emotions out loud, we see our friends standing in line to get in and Cindy is so excited she's where the action is that there is no getting through to her. My thoughts crumble into debris and I go back and forth from resentment to complete disgust with no love to be found in her presence. *She does look good, Neal, she does look good...* and this makes it a little more bearable to have her around.

Generic crew: Cameron, Alex, Craig from Chopper, and Sticky C are all standing in line too, so it kind of makes the whole experience rather repulsive. I take that back, as Craig isn't half as bad as the rest of them and he's even in a pretty decent outfit around these parts, even though their drummer's name does happen to be Shu.

When we manage to get inside it's so just outrageously loud, which is perfect as I can't hear Cindy squeak to Cameron about complete rubbish, even though I can still pick up bits and pieces of her typical convo about how she got *sooo* fucked up last night and how I came in and woke her up just a few minutes ago, and how she already can't remember a thing and how she wishes he would've been there asking him where he was and how she misses him and *blah-di-blah-di-blah-di-blah* and just the smirk on his face while she's yakking to him is enough to make me want to rip his face apart. We're just in time for the last local, which is fine because it all sounds the same to me and I just want the tour package to kick off anyway. So while they play lolly-gag on stage, I house four whiskey's and by the time Doobie O'Malley even gets on, I'm already a total slosh and I'm just diving off the stage like a five year old in a ball pen and honestly, I don't even know where Cindy is. By the time the set is done, I sober up enough and sweat off some of the drink and notice that I can't really find any of the guys anymore and that Cameron, Sticky C and Alex are not here, however I spot Craig leaning over on the bar smoking a menthol.

"Where is everyone?"

"The guys thought it was a bore. Took Cindy with 'em. She had enough anyways, she said."

"It's been twenty minutes! What fucking gives?!"

"Looks like you enjoyed yourself though," he says as he taps to my forehead, and as I touch it, I feel a cool spot of blood rush down towards my lips. *Just when did this happen?* I wonder. But right now, I just can't really care about this as I feel completely responsible for dragging her out here. I know that those guys know that Cindy is a loose gal and a broken wreck on all those pills tonight and even though I don't want to babysit, I'm going to have to play the part. But right now the band is on and the night is young and right before I kick off another two-step jig to the closer, I house a bourbon and continue to party.

MONEY AND THE DRUGS

There was that time when I felt on top of the world.

My blood, the royal juice oozing from Mount Olympus awaiting to be plucked and drooled over by vultures. Worshipped by those who fed off the surplus for years while my core essence supplied the nutrients for their well being. I felt immortal. There was a time I felt unstoppable. Soaring from the roots of the jungle, with my hands gripped tightly around the swinging vines, flying graciously from tree to tree in the depths of the Amazon, with Jane by my side. There was a time that I felt as if the world was flat and that I would be able to jump off the square end of the edge and dive into another dimension off into the waterfall of forever in which the underground became the society in which we all were made to function and swim in pools of silver lining and push the seal until my muscles began to bleed. There were a few times in which I was a king of my own colony (that's right, a *few*) making commands of the middle class to produce and sacrifice for my kingdom. I have been to the top of the world and had lunch with the sirs and tea with their wives and waged war on their uncles, and had biscuits to romp with their youngest daughters and have even been invited for seconds if I so happened to be interested or if I deemed the rendezvous necessary in the future. I know what it's like up there in the clouds with the women and the gold and the jewels and the money and the spa and the massage and the food and all of the other gluttonous desires conspired by those who have earned their right for freedom and gained a sense of empowerment over their fellow colleagues and had catered to their selfish needs. I have seen the beach and the outside bar where we got milkshakes and smoked cigars and wiped the kiss from our lips before we parted for what was essentially going to be forever and the last time I would ever see you again. There was never going to be a second chance.

Again, I go with the rant of the emotional appeal and how I dwell into the desert that is my mind. The wasteland of zero commute and low ethics that contrive empty cents and rips a hole in my pocket and drains the investment that enables me to flourish. The very feature that gives me the drive to love. The drive to feel. The particle that moves the joints in ways that gives us the power to win whole seasons year after year unaffected by the draft. With that I can say that I have seen the top. I have seen the top and we can talk about it only when you get there. The whole appeal of the top floor is a strict design of low influence in which everyone reacts independently in unison with their own personal accord. But I am back now and there is no going to and from it again. I have arrived with three cases of cold hard cash and have burned the bridges that hold the route together to return. The police cannot find us here. I know the way home and I have drawn a map of the trip including shortcuts and tips to align the directions. In case we would ever need to go back, you can count on me to be ready.

But I burned those bridges long ago and like I said, there was no going back to that now.

I have burned the gaps that connect that which was the very shackle of my past existence. The smiles were big and the times were ideal, but the memories ache with decay as a general sense of reflection is generated. I will take this money to the bank and I will buy the two of us a brand new method and plan of attack that will inadvertently create a new appeal to the way we live our lives. I am telling you, there is no going back to that which we once did come from. Although the events that took place will shape the shift that is to come, it is good to know that the tribulations of the past are now behind us, and the monsters are in the closet with the light off, shot and dead in the head behind the door.

Babyblack

Paul hears a sudden thud on the door. The sound of the key clawing to get in grinds in his brain. He knows who it is. *Fine*, he muses, as the noise turns into a heavy scratching and clawing, and it almost sounds as if a demon is attempting to enter through the gates of hell. He rushes off the couch to investigate exactly what seems to be happening, and surprise, surprise. It's Angelica trying to get in, borderline falling over with a little vomit on her lip, stumbling in her attempts to enter.

Paul had been living in the complex for a lean three months when he came down to the pool one day and saw Angelica laying out flat on her stomach with her top untied. The appeal was so graciously presented to him as she kicked her feet back and forth with black nail polish, upholding the neatest quarter-moon white strips of a pedicure at the tips of her toes. Her tan was as dark and deep as the tint on her Volcom suit, which made it seem as if she wasn't wearing one at all. Her blonde head with the black streaks was just about enough to make him drool as it glistened in the sunlight. She was a real fuckpet, he thought. Before Paul had set up shop in the lounge chair beside her, he went back to his apartment to grab a few beers and eyed his own reflection. *Not a bad score, Polio.* The she-tigress at the pool was his aim, and his goal was to make her realize who he was and that he lived there in confidence. It wasn't too long before they started chatting up a storm with her going off about her friends and how her like, oldest friend was fucking her best friend from high school, and how some girl she knew was starting to get a real nasty heroin habit, and how her student loans are going through the roof, and how she never plans on leaving here anyway, and pretty much just the sort of wankery that is contrived from the bag of coke Paul had found late in the afternoon just resting in his board shorts and his pathetic little six pack of heinie's. He, of course, was nodding in approval as if genuinely interested in her social conditions, but in reality, he just couldn't get over that paint job on her feet that kept etching for his attention.

Angelica was totally twisted from the start. Sure, Paul wasn't the ugliest of boys, but Angelica knew everyone was constantly checking out her ass and tits as she flaunted them E-V-E-R-Y-W-H-E-R-E she went, so it's safe to say that Paul was a mere contender caught into her twisted web of high confidence. She knew that if he didn't want to listen to her shit, she could find someone else that would. What made her think she could confide in him? Why was she sharing all these deep confessions regarding her friends to a total stranger? Could she trust his shit? The fuck was it cut with? Needless to say, Angie had a dozen Plan B packs back at her place in case situations just like this one spiraled out of control like they always did. With the whole atmosphere and progression from solo pool time to beers with the boy next door, to a surprise snort session with the shit, it was inevitable that she would fuck him. It just seemed to cap the whole experience. Everything would just sort of spiral in dog years. From a quiet afternoon relaxing, straight into a night of madness.

So they got to it.

Angie never told Cindy or Pam, or any of the other girls for that matter, about her relationship with Paul. It worked in her benefit that Paul had lived in her complex. It saved her a cab ride after the bars closed or a drunken journey through the night in her friend's H3 that she just simply adored. But since no one knew Paul and he just happened to be her neighbor, she could whore herself to him anyway she liked, with no repercussions towards her social circle.

Paul didn't mind, and in fact, was just slightly surprised that things turned out the way they did. He expected to have to work hard on her and would have to lay her lines of shit for days before she would come around. Now she was mixing up her apartment with his, trying to get into a bed to sleep in *and why not?* Paul thought, *I'm gonna fuck her asshole.*

Tavert Lounge Love

So we're both strangers but we both know we've been waiting for each other for a long long time and it doesn't matter what you're drinking and it doesn't matter if you're even drinking at all because right now right here it's you and me and we're waiting for the next thing to sweep us and take us to where we don't know but we know we want to go there together and even though I don't even know your name and even though we just met all of this could really not even be the case as you could be my best friend for the last fifteen years and I could be your boyfriend from the past but none of that can be of any concern to us now as I see you there standing just wondering why I am not making an effort to come close to you and introduce myself so that this may turn out to be the river city fairytale fantasy you have been brought up to believe will one day save you and sail you away into the night but this my sweet is not it and if you thought that we could mend this into an ideal reality just know that you are wrong because in this life doors get shut and lights get turned off and you will find yourself sitting there in the darkness waiting for someone to come take you and save you from your misery but deep down inside you know that isn't going to happen and all the faith and confidence you have in yourself will slowly start to whither away and even if you're becoming accomplished and making the most use of yourself and your time and the resources which have been made so conveniently available to you there is still a little voice inside your head that screams and pulls and begs you to stop and reconsider everything because right now and I can promise you one thing all I know is that you are making the worst decision you have ever come to terms with and even though you might claim to have the ability to come back I know what time can do to a person and I know how time can change things and even though you may think you will be able to just come back and act like nothing ever happened I can promise you that time will make sure to let you know that things have changed and even if you think none of this matters now since you are simply just so focused on getting as far away as physically fucking possible from everything you've ever come to know I can guarantee that a day will come where you will realize you have made the biggest mistake of your life and that this was the worst idea you ever came up with and nothing you could have ever done was going to get in the way of that and you weren't going to stop until everything you planned on leaving behind had changed and everything you were hoping to come back to had been ruined.

THE WHORE SON ROGUE
(THE ONE THAT ALMOST KILLS)

Confused? So now's about the time you begin to ask yourself, just what exactly seems to be going on here? Who are all these people? Just what exactly have they gotten themselves caught up in? Well my friend, I can assure you that all of this will soon be clarified. In case you were wondering who was who and what was what, I can tell you this and this for sure: Do not worry about what I am about to tell you. All your priorities and responsibilities; dish them out. You better be ready for the worst again my friend, because it's about to adapt into the room you are sitting in while reading this, to the bar you're working at while this unfolds, to the game you're watching while you turn the page, to the tv show that begs for your attention as you resume your focus. Slowly, I begin to consume all that is around you encapsulating the very world you are living in for the sole purpose of telling you this story and as the programming fades into an eerie static, the darkness that is my shadow becomes the stalking doom behind you, better yet, *the overwhelming dreary still...*

So, chameleon, now that we have you here, let us ask *you* a question. Again! How did you manage to sneak in here? What was the sole purpose of *your* intent? If the cause of mine was to tell you this and this alone, on what grounds do you feel justified in being here? Yes, I know the past is a strange, strange place, but just how the fuck did you manage to slide in through that keyhole? How exactly did you manage to negate all that's ever been done wrong? I look at you, I sing to you, I question you, but still no regard towards my query...

I understand and this, in fact, totally fucking get, but if I could excuse myself for one page turn and one page turn alone if you don't mind and please just let me, I will shove a fucking glass shard into your face just to make sure you cannot camouflage into any more of my scenarios, since as you know, nothing matches blood and blood stains all, and as you seem to be covered from head to toe in retro stoked like a bucket o'paint galore, I will spit in your face because this time, yes *this time*, I am going on this trip alone and can almost guarantee that I will not be thinking of you when I get there.

III. Lotions And The Nutrients

JUICE

Cindy wakes up on the floor and cannot seem to feel the left side of her face. She rises up, disheveled from her repeated attempts to stutter a whimper begging anything to give her a sign of where she is, how she got here, who she's with, and maybe gain an interest in figuring out where and what happened to Neal. She can hear laughing on the other side of the house and curiously gets to her feet and starts to walk towards the commotion. She wonders where her sandals are and why her feet are all black. There is a burn hole in her shirt, which she finds slightly odd since she doesn't smoke and as she opens up the door to the room with the giggling she sees a clock that displays a neon green 4:02. Craig is sitting upright with a red bandana around his head while Cameron and Sticky C both pass a mirror back and forth between them, each respectfully blowing a discrete line separated for the individual. The bright computer screen glimmers behind them.

"I need to go home, do you mind giving me a lift?"

"Why don't you call the lightweight, Neal? Kid can't handle his own!" says Craig as they all break into an uproar.

She doesn't understand why Craig is being so malicious or why he started snickering, but she could tell that she wasn't going to get anything done here. She knew the two didn't really get along with each other, and she wished she didn't act like such a bitch last night when she saw the guys at the show, blowing Neal off the way she did. She remembered how excited he was about the show and suddenly felt awful.

"What the fuck happened last night?" she begs to know "Where the fuck are my flops?"

"Honey, you were a total ride! We got you back here and Savage tore you up! You were talking all sorts of shit and we could hardly stand it so we left you two alone thinking the nights a boil." Sticky C bites into a Washington red and spits the saliva of the chew into a waste bin. Cindy hears the crunch of the apple and it disgusts her even though fruit is a pretty healthy substitute to a shitty pig breakfast. Cameron sits at the other end of the room laughing like a child at a sleepover pissing his pants for the third time snorting away at the glowing galore. When had she stopped remembering? Where was she to begin with? Why had Neal left her alone? Did he know where she was? Where was her cell phone? How did she get here? Could Craig be trusted? Where was Savage? *The pills must've fucked me again.* She asks Craig if she can use his phone.

"*Can I use your cell? I lost mine,*" Craig mimics and Cameron continues to laugh in hysteria. "Sure, but we didn't fuck around. Remember that."

She walks into the other room hearing the guys remain behind her snorting in laughter. Cindy calls Neal, surprised she knows his number, and squirms in agony at the thought of getting his voicemail, but he picks up and a wave of relief washes over her and if Atlas were to drop the world to his side for a quick cigarya, he wouldn't feel the fraction of Cindy's motions.

"*Neal…*" she quivers as she says his name.

"What the fuck, and who, and what do you want?"

"It's Cindy, I fucked up…"

"Where are you?"

She asks Craig the address, who screams it back from the other room. Five minutes later, Neal pulls up in his Wrangler blaring a song she remembers he told her made him think of her, for whatever reason he finds it appropriate. As they ride off into the cool afternoon, Cindy feels her stomach turn into a queasy, sickened guilt as she sits next to Neal in silence.

Investing In Our Futures

Cheryl Montana Fansdresser was delivered to Simona Kelly Monroe on September 24, 1982 in the height of the revolutionary ideology that C-sections were the new thing at 4:32 am in St. Mary's hospital in Jacksonville, FL. Amidst an emergency evacuation caused by a fire that started from a few tampons set ablaze in a waste bin in the ladies room, in which one of the nurses attempted to extinguish their clove cigarette in, she debuted herself on planet Earth emerging from the goo of afterbirth. Her father, Darren Daily Fansdresser was not in attendance due to a business trip that had him stationed in Sydney, and had he known that his wife would deliver two months prior to the expected date, he would have given his business endeavors a second thought.

Simona was an elegant lady of sorts. Having an extensive collection of porcelain dolls as a child, she naturally took interest in vanity and aesthetics in her adult life in regards to social delicacies. Late night banquets and participating in firm critiques of her honorary country club were her frequent community contributions. She was also becoming a frequent high flyer on Delta Air due to her stature with the executive males she frequently visited. This was all due to her exposure to the upper echelons from the brokerage firm she had partnered with in her mid-to-late-twenties. A company that provided her with a permanent seat at the Triple Crown Executive Suite at each airport she graced with her appearance. Simona graduated from a state uni at the young age of twenty-two where she and Darren had met at a nearby burger joint that had pretty lavish drink specials and took pride in having the best burgers in town. It wasn't after a summer went by when Simona found out she was pregnant that Darren, who was a rigorous playboy, took it as a sign to settle his ambitious libido and proceed with caution with his recreational approach to intercourse.

The two had moved uptown and purchased an admirable little condo where Simona was able to display her trophies from her younger years as a ballerina. Darren had picked up a second job aside from his daily role at the capital where he filed papers as an intern, and began bartending at a nearby Marty's from six to two in the morning. The couple had little time for one another besides the hours in between shifts, which would rarely call or allow for intimacy due to the long hours worked, and of course, Simona's thick condition.

A few months into the lease, Darren was notified that he would be going off to Sydney to promote a new pharmaceutical ingredient that would essentially toss glucosamine away from the forefront of joint therapy. A few weeks into the trip he had received a phone call from the Florida hospital notifying him of Cheryl's 6lbs., 7oz arrival. Simona had her neighbor, Raoul, drive her home a few days after the delivery. In Darren's absence, and her extensive lust for sexual conduct following the pregnancy, Simona also began having an affair with Raoul.

Darren, who was certainly not dumb and oblivious to these actions, found out about Simona's deceit very quickly, recognized that he was only twenty-three and was still a young, charming man and realized that this was not going to be where love remained and upon his arrival to the condo, evacuated the premises within twenty-four hours. Although livid at the thought of the mother of his child whoring herself at such an immediate pace after childbirth, he knew it was time to go. And it was natural. He left behind a rose for his former sweetheart, knowing that romance had died and the future for him was going to snowball into the everlasting. No one had ever heard from him again and Cheryl was turning out to be a bastard daughter with a revolving door for the male figures in her life to swing to and from in a leisurely fashion just as her mother introduced men into her life.

Simona maintained a surprisingly stable relationship with Raoul. First of all, he was her neighbor and was able to satisfy her needs at an alarming rate. Second, he managed to earn a profit off selling her and Darren's condo, to which no one ever said anything about, and thus allowed for her and Cheryl to move in with him a few floors below their current apartment and spend all of their money on leisure.

Raoul was a fairly stable man. Thirty-five and tan, Simona had always wondered why no woman ever found his irresistible charm which drew her to him. After all, this was what she found so appealing. She was worried that someone, somewhere, someday, might steal him from her. It was only a matter of time until this suffocation caused Raoul to distance himself from the now single mother and by the time he had thrown both Simona and her daughter out of the apartment, Simona had already established an awfully stable junk habit.

Simona was found dead in 1985 on a cold February morning in a one-bedroom studio on the corner of St. Bernard and Julius with Cheryl in a shitty Barney diaper crawling on the floor with no shirt on when she was just a little over two years old. The neighbors had complained of an awful smell coming from the third floor and the medics found Cheryl cuddling with her mother's stale corpse. No one had attended Simona's funeral.

Cheryl's foster parents would be all she ever grew to know and they offered her an extraordinary lifestyle that was better suited for a streamlined Hollywood heiress. William Sudazy and his wife

Ashley were total bombshells and since his cum was completely inefficient for Ashley's tubing, they had decided to adopt the runt from a local charity orphanage titled "Investing In Our Futures."

William, or better known as "Billy Boy" on his local commercials, was a Mercedes car salesman and owned a dealership on the south side of town. William and Ashley were social swingers and since Bill could never get anyone pregnant, his nine-inch dick was a real accessory at the gatherings. Ashley would often get in a furious, jealous rage and detest his intimacy with other women and fuck other men on birth control and always scream to the top of her lungs "keep it in fucker!" in order to inspire jealousy in her husband, although he never seemed to mind (let alone notice) as he was always the life of the party and knew his wife's selfish nature.

William's alcoholic tendencies ended his life on a summer afternoon in June of 1991 when he was driving from the beach after a swinger's party in Neptune. Drunk, he crashed his car into a post leaving $536,927,458.07 behind as of close of business in total investments, a 401k account in which Ashley was the designated beneficiary, a beautifully allocated 529 plan he had opened for Cheryl the day they had gained parental control over her well being, and an assortment of collectible cars and condominiums that were located all over the country.

Over the years, Cheryl began to detest Ashley. The two women were apart by nineteen years, and Ashley still looked like a fuckable item. In her teen years, Cheryl would bring boys home and Ashley often flirted with them to inspire a fuck and occasionally would snag and shag one, but it wasn't until Ben that Cheryl decided to liquidate the assets in her account and leave home taking a good portion of the lump sum left behind from her stepfather and committing to a glorious rental out by Jacksonville Beach and paying for it in full. Ashley was left alone and Cheryl never really minded to keep close contact with her stepmother. She had read somewhere that a BMW Z4, the same model that was her mother's, had crashed into a newsstand off Atlantic and Kernan, but she never really seemed to mind the details of the spread. She may have seen it on facebook and then quickly hid the news feed.

Cheryl never questioned the whereabouts of her family's presence and never really knew about the condition of her biological mother. Darren Daily was a successful business entrepreneur by now and had opened several restaurants in Florida in which Cheryl dined frequently. The two had even met on several occasions when he would be in the southern part of town for frequent meetings. However, with her tits being so pumped and her tight ass and lips being enhanced to a beauty (she had indeed blossomed into something quite the sight to see!) he did not see a trait of Simona in her figure. He had wished to grab her before and thought about pursuing the bachlorette on a few occasions, although nothing ever materialized.

Cheryl had met Ben at a Bruno's by the beach on July 4th 2006 when she was twenty-three and still in school and totally sauced on the tequila. Cheryl had a misguided approach to her conditions and had an all access pass hotel door key to the world. The money left behind in her account was so ridiculous that she could do whatever she wanted. It was only after a few years of dating Ben and living by the beach that she recognized that she was being abused by his grotesque demeanor. She realized what the values in this life were made of and decided to take a more recreational approach to her vast sum of money and began to exploit her glorious and sexual appeal.

Naturally, following suit with her biological mother and the fucked up nature of her horny stepmother, Cheryl gained a thirst for drugs that could only be quenched by a local screw with the dirtiest of cocks and the nastiest of appeals. Val was a real treat and it was only a matter of time before Cheryl was a depressed wreck all alone, with no family to turn to.

A Harder Piece To Work With

I scream your name until I am blue in the face, but it still gets nothing done. How the setbacks caused by our shortcomings and failures tend to bring us back down to size. You're still not anywhere near where you should be nor are you coming any closer to where you think you should be going. You can come closer now. Things have settled. I promise you we can make this work this time. But if you were here, would I just blow my fuse in your direction due to my inability to cope? Just how fair would that be? Sure my hair is longer, but does that make me any more of a man? My muscles have indeed gotten larger, and well, everyone says I can kill quite right, but just what exactly does that mean to us throughout the course of time? Should we truly be applying ourselves in any one given direction? Just what would it all lead to anyway? On whose standards are we even operating?

I believe that I was sent alone to scope. I have been brought down from the stars to take a good look and get a better understanding of what exactly is going on around here. I seem to produce. Sure. I seem to fail. Right. I seem to stand still. Ok. Does that mean I have come to terms with equilibrium? Is stable balance all I seek? Will I ever strive above the medium? Will I ever go beyond the average? What happens when I'll get to the top? Will I still continue to climb?

Do not tell me I will go below, for I have been there. I have scraped my knees on pavement, and my forehead stills scabs from the past when my face was flat down on the floor. I have fallen down and I have dragged beneath for way too long to not know what it takes to stand straight on my own two feet. But just what the fuck does this all come down to? What difference would the order of things make in any way at all? If I failed before, did I feel about it just as I would have if it were to happen in the future for the first time? I have seen, I have loved, I have been, I have went, I have gone, I have stayed. But have I truly lived? Do I convey my opinions in a way that is able to instill any emotion within you? Does the reader understand exactly what it is that I am trying to say? If this were to be spoken, and feel free to read the next few words out loud, would this make any sense to you at all? Does anybody else feel this way? Do we all come so close to fall short again? At what point are we able to gain the comprehensive retrospective that indicates we have truly succeeded and we no longer want to excel within our position?

So I come to you with this. I promise, and this goes to say if you will just let me, that I will hold you up with my own two hands until I can get us both to the top of that mountain. What we'll do when we get there is truly miles beyond me, and why we're going there, well, I can't really say. But I will tell you this, and I want you to listen closely, you can even find a private corner in the room to read this if you think that's necessary. The point is to get to the top together. The whole idea behind our success is to build a relationship that lasts. Maybe a few even. If we can get to where we want to go with others who are just as committed and like-minded, we will get to the top and be able to have discussions about it besides being selfish and egotistical in our approach to our wisdom of achievement.

To implement companionship we find, and I will.
But I scream your name until I am blue in the face, yet you are still gone.

DISCLAIMER

Susana busts into the room and Savage is laying on top of the covers, naked, still sleeping, snoring the zumba. The little bead dangling from the fan keeps clinging to the side of the uncovered bulb making a ting every time it completes a slow rotation. Savage had the tendency of not really caring about anything or anyone after finding out that he really wasn't like the rest of them. He took pride in his nightlife routine and was actually thrilled about avoiding the daylight and all of the negativity associated with the hours occurring on the other side of midnight.

"Get up, you pig!" Savage rolls to the other side of the bed neglecting the cries pleaded by his partner. He can feel the sheets underneath him being pulled and tugged, aimed at getting him off the bed, but nothing will get in the way of the eternal slumber. He can hear a slight nuisance coming from the room, however it's not loud enough for him to truly decipher what is going on. Something about running late, the mall, her girlfriend's birthday, homecoming, dinner plans, all a bunch of shit he could hardly give a fuck about, until it suddenly ceases, and the room is back to silence save the bead clinging to the bulb and a door slamming somewhere in the distance.

Susana was the only girl Savage ever found that was like him. They were dancing at a club on a full moon and he was looking for a score. As he came across the dance floor and into her sight, he recognized the delight in her supple skin. Aside from his absolute desire to tear through her flesh, he felt a slight resistance. As she played the part and escorted him to the ladies room where he would attempt to strangle her and take her out of the bar with him, she managed to actually put up a decent fight, and in her struggle she hissed a borderline growl and grinned two sharp cones on each side of her mouth, ignoring the heavy saliva pouring from her bottom lip. That night Savage knew he was not alone. They grew into a fully functioning relationship that was set aside from the boy's social circle, which led him to find confidence in knowing that there was somebody else out there just like him who he could confide in. All glory and good times aside, it was still an unfortunate disgrace for Savage, for as great as the sex was, Susana could not breed a child.

Savage was born Nathaniel James Edwards III to an old couple trying to get their family started in their late forties by birthing a newborn. His father, Nathan Edwards Jr. was born to a line of locksmiths dating all the way back to the beginning of the 20th century and his father, Nathan Edwards Sr. migrated from Ireland with his parents at the turn of the century to start the local business. His father, Nathanial James Edwards, could never be traced back to a point where someone could pinpoint the origination of the lineage, but all the relatives did know that there were myths of Silothian roots embedded into the bloodline of the family somewhere that traced all the way back to the 1400's. Regardless, the two were very distant and thought a child would bring back the love into their lives. However, the boy was born with a slight dilemma of dental hygiene and was born with a full set of sharp fangs, which caused the parents to be completely disgusted by his presence.

So just the opposite occurred and their newborn actually created a dark hostility between the two once they realized how incredibly unfit they were to be parents. This hate essentially leaked into poor Nathan who always felt a slight resentment in his presence. A few years with a background in troubled youth of violence with city kids aside an awful primary school education record led the boy to become hard. His father fled early in the boy's life, leaving him living solely with his elderly mother, which he was required to care for. The tribulations of his childhood are said to have established a thick coat of bitterness towards the boy's approach and calloused his emotional appeal towards the rest of the world.

Once he grew old enough to get a license and become mobile, he stole his mother's car and fled from Lansing, Michigan and planned to drive all the way until he hit Florida's first coast. The story goes to say that in between the trip from the Midwest to Jacksonville, Nathan got into an accident with a young couple who picked him up off the side of the highway, which caused their car to flip over killing them both instantly, while Nathan was left on the side of the road to fend for himself a few days over the age of fifteen. After walking about fifty miles away from the crash, Nathan stuck a thumb out to hitchhike and hopped in the car with an old man in a beat up Camry, that had a different color hood than the rest of the car. When he asked, the man said he was headed to Florida to kill his wife and daughter who had stolen everything from him in a brutal divorce. All the way down Kentucky and Tennessee stopping in all sorts of diners for quail and skunk meals, the old man continued with his rage for the two ladies, "Gonna kill 'em! I am gonna kill 'em!" until Nathan began feeling the old man's hate for his family. He couldn't understand why he resented them so much. Sure they took all his money, but who cares? He still had his health, right? Isn't a man capable, willing and able of doing anything he wishes to alone? All this talk about family, betrayal, and hardships led Nathan to reflect back on his family, and it was only then he realized, halfway through his journey through the country with a complete stranger, that he was never going to see his mother and father again. But they had no emotional connection to him. Sure his mother breastfed him as an infant and she depended on him to care for her, but there was no real connection, no *bond*. As the old man continued to ramble about the complications with his family and how he caught his wife fucking the neighbor's son one day and then took his daughter from him on the plus side as well as a court ordered settlement for half of his 401k and employee stock purchase plan from a regional finance corporation he had worked at for the better part of the last seventeen years, he began bursting into tears. Often laughing hysterically, Nathan began hating the old man. He was so sick of the pathetic bag of bones feeling sorry for himself and blaming his shortcomings on those two poor women. They probably weren't doing too well either, he thought, *fuck*. Setting himself up on such a wild adventure and being so trashed about it the whole time. There were people who had never left their neighborhood, and here was this complete scum getting tossed as he traveled down the states with his air conditioning and radio blasting. Nathan took immediate action somewhere in south Georgia and reached over the steering wheel and fought the old man off as they veered off the road and crashed into a billboard post. The old man had died on impact and when the medics arrived to extinguish the flames they had found Nathan unconscious bleeding from the lip and from the top of his forehead. The boy woke up three days later in a hospital with no recollection of anything. He had no means of identification and was miles away from home. The hospital found a foster family to care for him and Smith Lane, the neighborhood he was now going to live in, was full of beautiful young girls and swimming pools. Life was going to be pretty good, and Nathan felt that things got sorted out just right and placed right where they should be.

It was only into the first week with his new parents that they introduced their new boy to their neighbors. Nathan had a full head of blonde hair and a watermelon smile that was prepared by his foster family who were certainly well off enough to have his dental work completed. All the other mothers loved him, creating a jealousy issue for all the other boys in the subdivision.

One Friday afternoon the boys decided they were going to fuck his face up. They were tired of this newbie and of all the attention he was getting from the Ashleys and Samanthas on the block and how all their mothers continuously told them "why can't you be more like Nathan?" or "Nathan is going to be there, why don't you go?" and "you should sign up for football, Nathan is playing." Enough was enough and they had planned it all very carefully. No more was this red and white striped bathing suit wearing pretty boy licking candy cane lollipops by the pool wearing big green shades at lunch time going to walk through here like this. At his bus stop, they hid behind the mailbox and waited for the driver to pull away. Once he was past the street sign, Nathan felt someone grabbing the back of his book-bag, pulling him down. The boys had thrown him on the ground and began punching into his face. Two, four, six, eight, ten, twelve fists. Six people worth of might pushing into his big grin destroying every last one of his beautiful, ivory components that made him so delicious to look at. His face was on the melted pavement, sizzling on the cement in the heat of the afternoon. Getting pounded in the head by so many hands, thrashing at his gums, beating deep into his cheeks, mutilating the figure of his current face structure. Beating, beating, beating his head in to the bone. One of the boys produced a pair of scissors and had cut off all his hair leaving him with a grinning, bloody gum filled smirk and a retard haircut to a scratched scalp. One of the neighbors called his mother and it was right back to the hospital.

The parents did not go pick him up that night, feeling sick towards all the negative attention they were getting from their neighbors. Nathan's presence had created a vibe of hostility in the neighborhood that was grabbing at the claws of the street's positive atmosphere. Nathan stayed at the hospital by himself with no visitors for two days. He felt betrayed. He felt alone. There was not going to be a chance of love for him in this world. Something was not right here and if this was the game being played, Nathan determined to be the best. He had decided to go further than they could. He knew there were some things that were unforgivable and realized he was going to have to play along. He was going to mirror the behavior he had witnessed. He stole a pair of scissors and asked for a few dollars from one of the nurses and bought a hammer on the way home. Nathan was going to get both his teeth and his hair back.

He first started at Paul's. It was the darkest of nights and Nathan broke the window into the boy's room and jumped on top of him in his bed and began to beat him over the head, for what was to be about six or seven times with the hammer while he was still sleeping. This was just enough to make a gash in the skull and let oxygen come through, pretty much leaving the boy retarded. Paul was going to be disabled. *Perfect*, Nathan thought. Next he cut off the boys hair and stuffed it into his mouth as if he had a really hairy mustache that was getting in the way of his upper lip. Nathan looked at him and smiled. He dragged the boy into the kitchen and left him bleeding, whimpering softly and told him he was going to kill his mom and dad if he screamed.

He then went across the street to Jason's house. Jason was a real pussy, a complete potential pretty boy that would deserve no less. Nathan broke into the back door of the house and found Jason sleeping on the couch by his mother. His mother was a loose spin on over-the-counter drugs and assorted pharmaceuticals so she wasn't going to wake up and presented no issue. He had picked Jason up and carried him to the backyard where the moon created a spotlight to showcase the event. Nathan had swung the tool heavily towards his face and caved his mouth in with the back end of the hammer, essentially breaking off the boys jaw enough to become disconnected from the rest of his face. Nathan stopped and let out a giant sigh. He hit him once in the face with the back end as well, only for it to get stuck in one of his eyes to which Jason was crying miserably begging for him to stop. *"Why are you doing this, what is this? Please stop?!"* Nathan leaned over and flashed a gummy smile, "no, I won't stop, you want my look, get it?"

By the end of the night Nathan was so careful to hit the boys hard with an initial whack that they were unable to utter a word about their beatings. Finally, Nathan went home. His mother and father were still sleeping when he walked into their bedroom and he climbed on top of their bed and screamed "thanks for picking me up fuckers! I'm here!" following which he hit his father over the head with the hammer just hard enough to knock him out while he hit his mother in the mouth with such force, that it sent her two front teeth straight out of her face. Nathan had heard sirens in the background by the time he could even put the tool down.

Nathan was taken away in custody and placed under intensive care unit for juvenile offenders until he was eighteen. Nobody ever really wanted to befriend him due to his intense unstable nature and awkward looks since in reality, it was tough talking to a boy with no teeth. Almost tough to stomach the look on that one, really. Sure they were all violent, just not in such a creative fashion. Throughout the years of being detained, gaining a government sponsored education, Nathan's teeth began to reemerge into their twisted form and when he was released he would be unrecognized by those he wished to reach out and contact. Once the boy was released, he got a job working in a Creole kitchen downtown by the university where he managed to make friends and essentially roll into the social levels of college. It was only after a few semesters for the boy to get acquainted with a formal routine that would allow him to leak into the upper echelon of the highest quality of people and put himself in a position where he could get anything he wanted.

Savage throws the covers off his bed and sits at the edge of the mattress. It was hot and he could feel the sheets stick to his side. He rose to go to the bathroom and when he opened the door to his room he could already hear Susana getting the parts together in the kitchen for dinner.

To Steer

Dad always told me what was going on. He filled me in making sure I always knew what was happening and why and I never really thought about it twice until I got older. Meredith could have taken a hint from this and so could Pam who, I guess we don't need to mention, is miles away from any of us at the moment. It was always all this talk about aliens and how one day they're going to come down from outer space and take over and blah blah blah and who the fuck cares, lay off the drugs, as I always said. Or it could have been about anything else, really. If it's your job, who cares? I got mine to worry about. If it's your weekend, spare me, I've been busy. Is it your car? The payments are your fault. Fuck me if I never had the sympathetic ear to give a fuck. But I remember the years and the times spent alone and all the memories that have been established and I can't really forget the party last summer where we met and talked about that Alanis Morissette song where she keeps talking about how she got fucked over and how she couldn't stand having all of her lover's things over at her place after it was all over and now that I think about it, it's really not that bad of a song.

I think I'm failing my lit class. I can't remember the last time I even went. Is it time to enroll for next semester? Maybe I should look into it. It's been a while since I even looked at the curriculum. I think there should be a syllabus around here somewhere. How many years have I even been here? Isn't it time to almost leave? Should I be graduating this semester? I don't know.

I haven't talked to Chuck in a while. I've been so busy hanging out with this new clique, which isn't half bad. I heard Cindy got fucked up the other night. She left to go to that show we were all supposed to go to and ended up leaving with Craig and his crew.

From what I hear she ended up getting into a lot of trouble that night. That crazy pig Savage with the fucked up teeth ended up getting on top of her and Craig and Sticky C just stood there and watched, laughing. I wonder how this one was going to turn out, I mean, really. I wonder what Neal thinks about all of this. After all, I do think he loves her. Like old school sixteen-year-old loves her. Who knows. Who cares? I wonder what Angelica is doing. God, that bitch looks good. She just has the best face *and* tits *and* ass. I mean both of those are optional if you got that face. If you got a face that can kill a crowd you don't need tits and you don't need an ass, as I always say. Just mascara and lipgloss. At least that's how I always looked at it. Nothing is more attractive than a great big beautiful face and a huge pair of tits though. Fake tits. Nothing. I wonder if Val is around. I sure do miss him even though he is going pretty steady with Cheryl and he sure does seem to mind her quite a bit. It has been a few nights since we all have gotten together. I've just been so cold lately and when I tried calling home the other day, no one answered.

Johnny T

It sure has been a while since I heard from Pam. Last I saw her was when Samantha had me coming over freaking the fuck out over the gear she got sloppy with, and needless to say, she did look like fucking dog shit when I showed up. I had just dropped her off anyways, so who even knows how that managed to spiral out of control. But fuck it man, that girl was known for staying up three maybe four days at a time every week, so fuck all of it if it had anything to do with me regardless. Last I heard, Sam found a note she left behind in her apartment that she was going off somewhere, New York I believe it was, yeah, New York for sure. Fuck me if I knew what business she had going there, but I don't think Chuck even knew about it since that poor fucker is still in town. He's fucking Samantha, it's so blatantly obvious that *everyone* just *knows*. You know? What difference does it make, was I hiding my feelings for his girl? Regardless, it's weird she would just disappear like that, I tried calling her cell the other night one two three maybe four or five times even, but nothing. It's strange how people just have the balls to go like that, walk away, leave everything behind. Suddenly, they disappear. Lord knows I've been there. Shit, it was only a few years ago that I packed my bags and headed for the coast. I've been gone five years now and I haven't heard a squeak from the past since. Feels good to turn things around, start fresh, that's for sure. But man, Pam was such a sweet fuck, it was a damn shame she was gone. We sure did like to party. Fuck man, it was just the other night. I even tried to push it a little and thought about maybe going over to check out her apartment, and I did, but when I went over there and knocked on the door a few times hoping she would answer, I got nothing, just her dog barking which is strange since she did love the fucking thing so much it just doesn't make any sense that she wouldn't take it with her. When I asked Sam about it she mentioned that note she found by her front door that read something about how she didn't like the way things were snowballing and how her and Chuck were fucking up and ending regardless and all sorts of other shit. It was funny because when I asked her about the whole thing she didn't seem to mind it all too much and when I asked Sam to see the note she handed it to me and it was strange because it didn't look like Pam's writing at all, but fuck me if I can remember what her script looks like. I don't really seem to come around much anymore, I wonder if I too will fade. I seem to have lost an itch for company and for some strange reason, I feel cold.

Chuck Clarifies

I was smoking a cigarette when I reasoned with myself in regards to what I should do and it all suddenly became very clear. I was to destroy the bodies and take Pam on a little trip. Since no one was going to stop looking for a five-foot-seven-fuckable-blondie it was evident she had to go somewhere. Carl was no big deal since he was a loveless online predator. He could hide in the backyard for months and no one would even know about it. So he's gone, dead, buried, forgotten and peed on. When Tara asks about him we can just deny everything. Right? We can do that, okay? The two of us weren't associated in any way, so it was an easy fix. Pam, however, was going to take a little more effort. I would for sure be in the spotlight. After getting both her and Carl out of their respective ditches, I began to hack at their arms and legs into little pieces and buried them in scattered locations throughout the backyard. Only then did I notice how much property this rental had. No big deal. Stay cool. After meticulously cleaning EVERYTHING and even burning a little bit of it with the gasoline I brought over from earlier, I went inside to write a little note on behalf of Pam. She always talked about going to New York and how she had family there and how it would be so fucking great to just go there one day and check it out. Fine. Here ya go. You're fucking there. I drove her Civic back to her place and threw the note by her doormat and got on I-10 and drove all the way to the other side of the state. The ride was pretty creepy, just driving in the darkness of the night in my dead girl's car knowing she was buried in separate pieces throughout my lawn back home. I felt pretty morbid for a minute, but just a minute and I stepped out of it and snapped back real quick and kept staying focused. When I got into town I stopped in a waffle house and got some smothered covered hash browns. Wade, a good friend of mine, still happened to be working the graveyard shift and he served us right and it was good to see that he was doing well. From there, I parked in a greyhound station and scratched the vin number from the dash and took the plate off the back bumper. I bought a ticket back into town that night and left at approximately 3:50am getting back home at just a little after 7:00. The fucked up thing was that I left Pam's phone in my bag for whatever reason, and she must have gotten at least seventeen calls from that total spook Johnny or Johnny T or whatever the fuck these whores were calling him these days. I was feeling pretty fucking brave about the whole thing, since I had effortlessly managed to move her car miles away and conceal the deal and when I walk in through the door Tara is sleeping on the couch with Darla in her lap.

MILKSHAKE

Paul and I are going to get milkshakes and it's almost like, I don't know, midnight? Sure, whatever. I got a call from Cindy earlier but she was a total bore. Telling me all this awful shit about what happened to her the other night that she herself doesn't even remember but somebody, she said, had told her all about it. Apparently she doesn't seem to mind the details of anything that happened to her. Neal was real pissed, I know that for sure. He called me the other night to complain but I could totally give a fuck less about it. He spent the majority of his six o'clock that night telling me all the fuck about it. *Apparently* they aren't talking. Whatever, it's not me he's fucking. Paul is looking good though. He's got that new haircut from that cute girl at the mall who knows how to handle her razor and I've gotta give it to him, he does look pretty fucking shagalicious. I haven't heard from Pam at all. That bitch Samantha keeps calling me and fuck me if I even know where she got my number. I don't seem to understand how that kind of shit just floats the fuck around. But things sure have gotten sloppy. It has been a few nights since I've seen any of them. Cindy has been out on the rag getting stream-rolled through. Pam is totally MIfuckingA and Neal is being fucking Pinocchio and Johnny T has been a miss as well who's a total creep anyway but knows where to get the best shit. Good thing I have Paul to rub me down. Good ol' six pack at the pool. Gotta love that fucker. We pull up to a Sonic's and I order like fourteen dollars worth of shit that I hardly even look at but Paul pays anyway and eats some of it. We go back to his place where we get drunk and make a fucking mess and just before we pass out and fall over on the living room floor, he picks me up and totally drills my asshole not even getting at me regular at all and I look in the window and see my reflection, blinds up, not giving a fuck about the neighbor across the field of condos, and see that anal doesn't look any different and I still look sexy as fuck and when I look up I see Paul has lit one of my Marlboro's and even though he ashes on my back a couple of times the whole deal just totally gets me wild and I think I lose myself about six or seven times before I wake up the next day on the floor beside him sore as a dead dog and I feel awful about everything and I can hear my phone in the distance somewhere but Paul has his arm around me so tight and even though I am dead tired and totally uncomfortable I just lay there, like a corpse fully awake smelling and feeling like shit and realize that there is just no way Pam went to New York. There is just simply no fucking way.

REALLY, BEAUTY QUEEN?

Right when I got to Pam's I knew something wasn't right. Her car wasn't there even though she told me she was going to leave Chuck's house early in the morning and we would go to the beach for lunch today. Since I know she's fucking Johnny anyways there isn't a chance in the world she would want to stay another night over at Chuck's house, *even though I totally wouldn't mind that* but it was all going to work out just great. But for whatever reason, this just didn't feel right. I went by her door looking for anything; a key, an unlocked window, but all I found was a note, looking all cryptic, scattered, shakey, not like Pam's handwriting at all.

> *If you want to find me, I have left for the better. I'm off to New York where I told all of you I was going anyway. Go ahead and hate since you think I'm a bitch, but the day to leave is today. Smooches!*
>
> *XoXo Pam*

This was weird. Smooches? I don't understand. I call Chuck, maybe he knows where she was, but certainly he doesn't answer. I drive by his place thinking she might be there and see his car there. When I knock on the door nobody answers and I can see his hippie roommate sleeping, laying on the couch with that fat fucking cat in her lap. Times like this I wish that Val never really got serious with that Cheryl skank, that way I would have been on the outside circle with him looking in with twisted eyes pointing, laughing and making funny gestures at all our stupid shit. Maybe she did go to New York, who knows, but I mean we were just talking last night about how we would go get our heads straight and get some fresh air after we both graduated. Did she want me to go with her? What the fuck Pam, this just doesn't make any sense! I mean, after that incident with Johnny T I thought she may be a loose peg but seriously, this is pretty fucking extreme. Especially if she drove there? I mean fuck man, that's like a two-day trip *easy*. I try Angelica, who I know is a total cunt and can't stand me either, thinking maybe she knew something since her and Cindy were always going out with Pam to ladies night at Bango's and getting caught up in no good nightlife, but she didn't answer either. Fuck, what is the point of this stupid phone? I'm totally fucked and slipping and no one is answering and Chuck is gone and Pam is gone and I'm pretty much all out of options and just then I think that I should head up to the pool. On my way I call Johnny, which I figure might be a good idea since he might know a thing or two about Pam's whereabouts, but he says he hasn't heard anything and when I tell him about the note, he finds it kind of strange and the phone goes into a deep silence for what feels like a half-hour. I hang up and figure I'll just have to wait for Chuck to get back, even though it's really strange that his car was at his place and he wasn't there. I did try calling his phone a few times again later and hoped I wasn't looking desperate. Right around the time I make another attempted phone call, I feel my tampon slide out and realize I haven't changed the fucker in almost twelve hours.

What Happened To Meredith

"Why does everyone think she's such hot shit?" Cheryl stares Val down condescendingly.

"I mean, everyone's got those tits, Doctor Palmer has just been fucking *plugging away* out there by Southside, sure like, *yeah*, her face is alright, but what the fuck were you doing with Chuck nailing her when Pam walked in? I mean both of ya'll? You have fucking hpv you sick retard." Val wasn't exactly the one to sensibly debate with in regards to what anyone was doing or who was watching when it was happening, let alone mind a thing or two to talk about in a situation pertaining to him or his buddies. "I don't know why you're acting like this, like, like a little bitch," Val utters but before he can come to terms with his lover and generate some sort of compassion so that she can forget about the intricacies that make Val the man he is, he is suddenly shoved, plunged, pried and torn open as Cheryl sticks him with his Benchmade black-grip so deep that her hand enters the gaping wound. He is pushed against the wall and cannot pry Cheryl a distance of two feet before he is slipping, using the wall as guidance, making his way down unto the floor. Cheryl keeps pushing and pressing against his stomach as if to force a deeper entry but before she pokes deep enough to go through to his vertebrae she looks down at Val as if to provide some sort of sympathetic grin to the whole situation, but he just lurks into darkness as his ability to understand the physical weakens, and he is left laying dead with his head in her arms, eyes coated black. Cheryl began to sob silently while she sat on the floor covered in Val's dirty, dirty, black blood. Interestingly enough, she suddenly began thinking about the times Ben would sneak into her house early in the morning after he was out drinking with Craig and Shu and instructed her to put the blonde wig he had bought for her as he would so viciously rip through her blouse and make his way into her asshole. *"We're going to call you Meredith..."* he would utter as he pried her ass cheeks apart and made his way in and between her thighs and Cheryl never really knew why. Poor Cheryl just rising out of deep slumber in the early hours of a weekday morning being forced into role-play. She knew Ben used to chat with 1800-GET-FUKD about two or three times a month, so whispering crazy shit was just something she understood he was into. But now she was all fucked. Her Baby was murdered by the scum she just freed the earth from. And now, yes now, she was all alone. What was left to do besides mourn the loss of the social life? How truly, truly Shakespearean.

IV. Catastrophe Call

Control, *wait...* Control!

At Cameron's drinking with Coleman and Phil, we wait for the guys to get back from the show while watching a porn that Sticky C left behind at Coleman's last Saturday when he blacked out over there after that total faggot party at Chuck's that was a total slop house, which had so many dicks at, that a whore wouldn't even know what to do with. I rise to get another beer and am simply in a total fuck when I spot that there is no more booze in the bottom of the fridge and am urged to freak since I only got three out of the eighteen I had brought over. But just as I pry my lips to yell at the two lightweights in the den, Cameron pops in screaming up a fucking storm and a few of the guys trail him. We all rally up and give a slightly tense welcome but my eyes gaze into one direction and in one direction alone as I spot the Bella being escorted with eyes in the back of a blonde skull. As the fellas sense my heated approach in her direction I hear Cameron echoing in the distance *"no man, she's cool, ease off bro,"* to which I respond a firm fuck off as I haven't gotten a fix here in quite some time and am looking to end what I would personally like to consider, a really shitty fucking streak now. Mind you, the girl is fucked, and I mean *totally* fucked. I've seen her and her girlies around at the union minding their shit looking like a bird just waiting to be tossed at a distance becoming ever more appealing as you draw nearer and nearer until you suddenly grab it and right before you squeeze it so fucking hard as if to pop the eyeballs right out of its head you realize that you could fuck this thing and right then as you violently begin to thrust and push and aim to destroy the very essence of the most beautiful creature you have ever touched the guys are in the background egging you on shouting *"fuck yeah! get her deep!"* to which you finally cool off and realize the repercussions of your actions and even though it feels so good and the girl is practically a dead beat scum fucked up on the prairie line in the bottom end of a dried up well, you know that deep down, you're going to have to finish or something about this whole thing just wouldn't be right. *It's all or nothing fuckers!* you think to yourself and even though you can still hear Cameron and Sticky C laughing like hyenas in the elephant graveyard you are not motivated or driven by their presence, but instead are driven by your animal nature to consume, destroy, repeat but for some reason are still slightly moved and aroused by the presence of their inappropriate company and as your fangs began to purge from your tender gums you reach in to bite, but right before you squeeze the skin on the girl's neck with your teeth you shoot a load deep inside that has the tendency to sprout a being who will grow to be similar in nature.

MIXING CORDIAL EFFORTS

So the ride back home was a total mind fuck even though it was hardly what I needed after last night and I knew Neal was probably fucking morbidly, vividly, epically super turbo pissed at me even though he had no real reason since, after all, it wasn't him that filthy pig Savage fucked even though I did end up leaving him at that show. I smelt like shit and that stupid fucking song he always blasted when he was real blue was blaring at the height of his speakers and I really wish I could have gotten anybody else to come scoop me, *anybody*. Shit, even my fucking dad would have been better than this, but I couldn't get a hold of Angelica and I hadn't heard from Pam in a couple of days and I didn't really know what happened to Neal after I left the show last night anyway so it only made sense to give him the courtesy of calling and getting him to pick me up from Cameron's. Regardless, I look just absolutely god awful and cannot wait to get home to wipe off this bullshit from my face and clean off the makeup that has so miraculously made its way down to my face and chin and made me look as hot as you can possibly imagine, like that one pornstar in that film Cameron had playing at his party that night, that Coleman apparently stole from one of his friends where the girl has so much spit running down her mascara-soiled wet face from blowing I think it was seven dudes and looks into the camera and says *"I want to be a super freak!"* in a begging and really awful manner that is still somewhat slightly seductive and it almost makes you feel sorry for her *and say fuck, where are the parents in all this?* but for some reason the whole situation makes the scene even hotter and the fact that this twenty-something is being treated like a bag of meat is really something to speak for, and it's kind of kinky actually and I can see why the guys would like this. Halfway through the drive Neal starts screaming about a bunch of ass, which in all honesty is probably shit that concerns me that I should be listening to since he is rather bright and does have a firm footing on things, a lot more than I do that's for sure, but this time I think he's really lost it but I'm still trying to listen to him and pay attention and give him the respect he so rightfully deserves, but for some reason I can't, and my mind is in like a million and five different places at once and I can't really seem to focus on anything else besides that cumulative test that I have on Monday in my prehistoric lit 3012 class that I haven't even cracked open a fucking speck in a book since the first week of the semester. Needless to say I was fucked from both ends. By the time Neal drops me off at home (he hadn't said a word in over twenty minutes after we got some grub over at Mika Mango's which was really awkward *to say the least* as we both just fucking sat there in silence with our shades on not saying anything to each other) it's almost five o'clock. I get into the house and luckily none of the girls are in so I don't have to explain my bukkake appearance and I take the time to get into the shower, but not before I put my iPod into the dock and blast Rufio's original classic me and the girls on the track team used to jam out to back in high school in '03 and when the water is just hot enough to get in I take my panties off and remove my bra and as I climb into the tub real slow, watching my every step, an inseparable desire to die takes over me and I feel so completely worthless and empty and gain acceptance of the fact that I am just so full of shit and everything I have ever done and everyone I have ever known was a lie and a fake and realize that my entire life has been accumulating to this and that this was something that was so far away from anything that I had ever imagined or wanted and I begin crying hysterically and find myself huddled into a ball on the bathroom floor soaking wet shaking in hysteria at my current shortcomings, and just before I come to and settle my blood flow I wonder about all the wrong turns anyone has ever taken and wonder what would happen if everyone followed the wrong way in regards to where they were going, and that there might be a slight chance that maybe, *just maybe*, they would find people who were like-minded when they got there, and that in the end, things would be alright.

SPOILED DIRTY ROTTEN

Darla rises to the sound of the door creaking open and this causes Tara to notice Chuck in the front of the house putting his key to unlock the front door. Chuck walks in through the room, *looking like shit*, Tara thinks, *but hey, I'd still fuck him* and as he makes his way to the couch and puts his feet up on the table she notices how dirty his shoes are, almost as if he ran around in a muddy tailgate. The floor has been molded into complete slop trailing him in from where he came. Tara looks out the window and sees his car, surprisingly wiped completely sparkling clean. Chuck turns on the tv and quickly falls into a deep haunting slumber and begins to snore so loud that Tara has to get up off the couch and go into the other room just to fade it out even though she realizes it is already a little after seven so she might as well get her shit together and get ready to go to her job at the Tienka Market where she sells incense and pogs in her shitty fucking booth that averages about forty or so dollars and some change every weekend. While Tara is in the shower, Darla makes her way out of the window and out into the backyard. She starts to dig up compound, getting her face entangled in clammy dirt and placing her paws in, then out, and right then left into the ground that her face turns grey from the grass and soil. Once Tara gets out of the shower and spots her cat in a frenzy, she looks to the soil and realizes it to be slightly disheveled. *I don't remember the ground being so moist and tender* she thinks as it almost looks as if a landscaper brought in new dirt for a family to garden. Tara pisses off this detail and scoops up Darla and brings her back inside. She notices Chuck is still on the couch sleeping and takes a second look at his shoes from a distance and doesn't mind to connect the mud with the soggy ground she just spotted. Tara goes back into her room and attempts to call Carl for a quick fuck since Chuck has been so busy with Pam lately and has also been rather distant, and being a patchouli oil grease trap doesn't really give you a fuck to worry about when an individual is tangled in a web. To her surprise she receives a continuous ring in the distance and realizes that the phone is actually inside the house. Chuck rises from the tone and recognizes the jingle and his eyes bulge in an epic circle as he thinks *thank god, it was all a dream, that fucker is still alive and well and here* but Tara goes into the kitchen and grabs the phone and asks Chuck "when was Carl here?" to which he just closes his eyes as a neglectful response and as he looks down to the floor to spot his dirt tracks from the front door he sees Darla playing with what looks like a ball of blonde hair.

The Terribly Selfish

Cheryl's millions meant absolutely fuck-all now that she had the guilt of a serpents coil in her stomach right above her upper pussy area. Sure, she had the money to get away with the act, she saw how the jury sympathized with Val's case and how easily the lawyers made him out to be such a saint when Ben was damn well sure in the right when Val chibbed him. She knew what she could get away with and it really didn't take much for her to paint a self defense case against Val's death indicating that he in fact had forced her into submission, anally penetrated her against her will, leaving her with the only option to stab him repeatedly to get him off her. One of the jurors was so convinced and moved by the case and what Val's actions had caused Cheryl to do that he took the initiative to establish a scholarship in her honor for girls who are mistreated in college and need special aid to get through turbulent times. What a total fuck all. It took a few weeks to get the kinks sorted but Cheryl was sleeping every night in endless rollovers tying knots with her duvet being left all alone. Death and misery had been all she ever knew since she was born, losing everyone from her foster parents to her friends, and now that everything had settled she felt absolutely fucking morbid. She stayed in the house for the better part of the following spring season and lost damn near thirty pounds shedding tears of pain.

It was a Saturday night and Cheryl realized she couldn't sit in the house any longer. She got into the shower and blasted the new Margot and the Nuclear So & So's album to extremes and listened to the whole thing, front to back, while under a steamy rain of pressure massaging her back. When she got out, she looked at herself deeply in the mirror and looked straight into her black eyes. *You're invisible, you god* she said to herself and as she turned away into the hall and made her way to her room to get ready she made the decision to go to extremes on this particular night, pushing envelopes if you may. She found her tight black dress that she knew made her ass look *sooo* and her tits ab-fab and applied a thick coat of mascara and penciled around her lids real dark, a heavy line of black. She straightened her hair out for the better part of eight to nine o'clock or so and drank a few glasses of bv-cab in the process before her taxi arrived well into the better half of ten pm or so and by the time she even tripped over the first step out of her condo and into the ride, she could barely utter the direction but the driver understood where she was going and off they went to Mika Mango's where her and all of the thousands of girls that looked just like her were going that night since Purgatory from 10-12 is well underway and even though the drinks are small, shitty, watered down, and take about twenty or so minutes to get (and for the $10 cover it's a total mindfucking rip-off), it just so happens to be the one legitimate place where girls like her can roll around like cattle and find somewhere to go later and get fucked.

Story Car

"So you're looking fine this evening young lady! I guess I know where you're off to! No worries, I'll make sure you get there safe. Made a few rounds out there earlier this evening, you know, definitely a hot spot, mind you. Never been there myself, personally not big fan of Mexican, or fruity drinks for that matter. Always been more of beer guy, you know? But I guess the company is something to speak for. Oh man, I love this song, you ever heard these guys?" Cheryl is about to vomit in the backseat of the cab as the driver's voice is making her ill enough to wonder about anything else besides the bullshit spewing from his uneducated filthy mouth that displays a few missing teeth. *You drive a cab in a fucking college town, you idiot* but she knew better than to let that shit spill no matter how fucked she got. The car finally stops and Cheryl feels as if she can finally catch her breath. "$32.50 gorgeous," she slaps the faggot two twenties and wonders off out of the cab as Esteban is left staring at her left cheek that is so conveniently hanging down the bottom of her short skirt "*the dirty, dirty fucker*" he mumbles to himself, slurping drool off his bottom lip as he tugs his cock within his pant leg and drives up and away, deep into the dark street.

Cheryl stumbles up into the patio of Mika's. The crowd is pretty generous and the band is playing its typical 80's nonsense even though it is supposed to be cinco here year round. A few guys escort her to the bar and she just pushes them off grunting an annoyed mumble. Everyone leaves her alone since she can barely keep her eyes open and no one very rightfully wants to be held responsible or be left accountable for that matter, but to the county's surprise Chester the bartender is so preoccupied taking orders that he irresponsibly serves her a straight vodka (which she so respectfully ordered) even though she's sauced beyond repair. She downs the drink and makes her way to the bathroom where she loses about three to four pounds throwing up the sushi she had for lunch and maybe the pretzels she ate for breakfast into a shitty toilet in which a bloody tampon swims in a few circles around a nugget. After hurling deep into the porcelain, she makes her way back out into the dance floor and feels someone grab her wrist. Not too hard, but strong enough for her to recognize that she is in fact being grabbed. "My name is Johnny, baby, where are *you* going?" to which she makes an *I don't know who you think you are buddy, but I can tell you who the fuck I am* face, but she, for whatever reason, only feels natural and for some reason obligated to play along and even though she can barely keep her eyes open, they're dancing together to *Do You Remember The Time?* then to Journey following which ZZ Top and the new Phil Collins single play and then back to Journey again. She pushes herself towards him and places her lips on his and begins to lavishly make out with this complete stranger, sloppy, drunk, tongue out and all. The man had so generously offered to drive her back to his place for a few drinks that it only made sense for her to tag along, and she did so before last call was implemented. On the ride back home Johnny blares tunes that are so foreign to her innocent ears with blaring keyboards and soaring melodies and she really seems to fucking dig the jams. "This is Molotov The Gym Rat, just came out with a new one, *totally* fucking sick, just listen to this!" and before you know it Cheryl is playing darts in the boy's living room with a gin and tonic in a tall glass and can sense that it is only a matter of time before they fuck each other, and I'd be a liar if I didn't indicate how bad she wanted his dick inside her. It had been so long since she was out of the house, let alone touched a throbbing Johnny. The boy excused himself generously and told her he was going to use the bathroom. *Perfect* she thought, I'll just sneak in right behind him and pull his cock out. But this was different. This was something completely foreign to sweet, sweet Cheryl. Johnny was sitting on the tub with a spoon and a lighter heating up what appeared to her to be cocaine. *What the fuck?* she quietly mumbled, but the boy was so caught up in his project that he didn't even realize that he had company and that his privacy had been intruded upon. "Oh shit! Close that fucking door!" he blurts out in excitement when he finally realizes Cheryl is standing right behind him. It was almost as if this was something that he did. As if it was a part of his game. As if the *oh, pardon me while I go to the bathroom even though I'm actually going to cook me up a shot* excuse was a part of his deal, since he knew girls natural instinct is curiosity to figure out what is going on and then essentially become a part of it. Pathetic in a sea of dwell, Cheryl knew his heroin was terrible. *It fucking looks like cocaine.* She had been down in the bottom and knew her shit and had now become hopeless and defeated. "I want to try..." Cheryl pleas but Johnny doesn't let her and a few minutes later he is blacked out on his bed and Cheryl is left chain-smoking cigarettes on Johnny's front porch too fucked to call a cab.

GET FUCKED

It's been too long for us to consider anything of what could have been or what could have happened to her but the past is here to haunt us and at the end of the day she isn't fucking here. We miss her voice. Miss her face. Miss her around getting us excited for the next thing coming our way. We realize we can't possibly stay cooped up in the house anymore and come to terms with our reality and recognize the fact that fresh air will only separate the nostalgic from the newly born. We rise, we wash, we grab the keys and before we know we're out on the street making our way down to the local tab that we'll soon open and bow before. The atmosphere feels warm and creates an ease to mold into the elusive environment that is the fresh aroma of the outside. Eyes bulging through a curtain of eyelids, we make our way through the sea of sweaty arms and hair that's been glued to bare backs and titties that have been banged out through the tightest skin and leather. We're pressed tightly up against the wall with our drinks in our hands side by side making our every effort not to melt away into the ooze of this cryptic night. We spot a young, trim, tan looking thing making its way towards us. Could this be a 1990 baby? Just as she passes us by, rubbing her chest up against our arm, we grab her by the wrist and when she looks back at us when can tell she is almost totally fucking gone which for some reason seems to make the whole thing work and yeah the 80's blare in the background and we both laugh real hard when we realize we hate the song and even though we strive to make an effort to recognize each other but cannot as she is every girl we have ever seen and we are simply at a loss as to why she is willing to coincide with our efforts and approaches towards her, we dismiss any misconception of denial. This fucker has been hooked. And as we dance and rub and grab and squeeze and slip and slide and tug and pull, we feel the beat of the rhythm grab our hearts behind our ribs and as we embrace into a deep kiss in the middle of the floor between hundreds of others who feel just as we do who are all just as lost as we are, we know the responsibility of the night and how the addiction has us hooked to do things against that which we strive to achieve and even though we're so excited to branch out and find a new beginning we know what we must do and how the night must end. 1990 baby makes every effort to stick to us throughout the night and as we make our way out the bar, we have her on such a tight hinge that she throws us a few bucks for the ride to the house and when I get there and rush to the head and cook up the lot, '90 baby interrupts and bulges in as if proclaiming a disclaimer on a soapbox but *as the liquid sips in and the agony escapes my lungs* our eyes fade into thin sheets of darkness that flow through an epic dilemma of interference when we realize the doll won't be having any of this and she'll be sleeping on the couch tonight and when she rises in the morning there'll be plenty of explaining to do but the sickness has us hooked to such a high degree that even though we know the consequences of our actions and are aware of the brutal strength of our shortcomings the rise before the fall feels so good that we neglect the outside and put the worst inside us. "No, *you can't...*" we mumble to the baby in every effort to practice safety and precaution, responding to her desire to taste the inevitable. But we've failed us. We've failed everyone. Our parents, ours siblings, our friends, our sons, our daughters... We have fallen apart. And now as we come to terms with the fact that as an individual we did in fact fail, and struggled all in the process of our efforts to overcome, we can't find the good or validity in anything we've ever done.

We see the girl go outside in a fury blazing smokes back and forth repeatedly. We feel bad and think *we could've loved this one, could've made it work* but we're so blue and so fucked beyond repair and so far away from the one we miss more than anything in the world that there simply is no explaining this. If only you told us why you left. If only you talked to us about it for a second. Couldn't you have just mentioned it in the slightest bit? We're so lost without your love. And now that we're here on another one of those fucking nights where everything will be left feeling skewed and guilty from start to finish, we fade. This time we fade so hard and so far that it takes us back and we can't rise. No. This time, we can't rise. This time, we are taken to another dimension *the simple concept of trust, you can't take back some mistakes, you've come to see me now I know that my life must end.*

WEST 33RD STREET

At the end of world, if I could afford to send out invitations, I would make sure to include you, my friend. On top of my cordial efforts, I would make sure to remind you to rsvp for the festivities and the abnormal amounts of congratulations the entire party would receive. The end would soon be near but we would be enjoying ourselves together for one last time to such a high degree that even death could not amount to. On this special night, nothing would get in our way. An intervention of the aforementioned. An intricacy of the most delicacy. An effort spent on the most gracious compliment. Eat and dine and sing in line and swing and shout and scream and pout but fuck me if couldn't tell you now, keep your drink in order. The view from where I stood was pretty badly morbid and the sounds from where I lay were certainly an effort to the most complex of individuals imaginable. We will get into details soon enough about the gruesome display of horror that took place, but before we dig deep (and by deep, I mean *deep*) let me express my love to you, beautiful one. To the face I love the most, to the voice that I cherish, to the sounds you display, to the sight that you are, to the distance between us and the details that drag between everything you ever told me over the phone, in person, face to face, in letters, postcards, texts, emails, smoke signals and any other form of human communication that would let me know how it was that you felt about the past, the present, the future and the nearly damned, I thank you now in advance for the application of your communication. We are the remains of an attempt at explanation. We are the ruins of history left behind to rest in rust and remain being rained upon. We are the artifacts of time coated in dust and left behind to spoil. We have been turned inside out from the coated failures of our pathetic attempts to prosper. There is no going forward. There is no catharsis. There is no beginning to a learning curve and no sway in direction for the future to mend. We are destined to fail and the attempts of our fathers have led us to a future that provides absolutely zero benefits of growth and amendment. At the end of the day when you lay in bed and realize you cannot fall asleep due to the heavy burden left behind by guilt and depression, remember that certainty is yours and yours alone and that no one else can take the facts away from the story teller even if in fact the story teller is a menace who refuses to tell the truth.

SILENCE BETWEEN

I didn't even wait for Cindy to make it to her front door before I took off. I certainly did feel like an asshole about it later though, not that it really matters, I mean it wasn't her fault those guys were dicks, but then again she did leave with them. Fuck me, I don't know man. My whole attitude towards everything that happened is so fucked. Now should be the time to console Cindy, tell her everything will be alright, that I'm there for her, *that we'll get through this.* But I don't think I can do that. I don't think I can be that guy. When she got in the car earlier she looked like a bag of meat. The beautiful girl she had been just a few short hours prior to that was totally gone. I was grossed the fuck out man, I don't know. When I got home I called Angie but she didn't pick up so I sat around for the majority of the day smoking pot and swimming laps at the pool, that surprisingly nobody was at which was weird since it was a perfectly sunny day. When I got back to the apartment to shower off I put the new 311 release I bought at Stripped CD's earlier in the week into the stereo and blasted the fuck out of a few solid tracks since the album turned out to be quite a worthy listen even though they've been around for years and it's really all the same shit over and over and over again. In the shower, I turn to face the cold water on my face in attempts for it to rinse my disgust away and down into the drain. I towel off and dress in casual attire, freeballing jeans and sporting flops as I grab my keys off the counter. I figure I'll go get some drinks and waste away this shitty day. I hop into the jeep and head down to Mika Mango's where I have about seven and a half house margaritas doused with Grand Marnier that only tends to make everything better. But it doesn't, and as I get deeper into the bottom of each glass and the grains of salt crush between my teeth, I start to resent my disgust with Cindy and realize I should probably call her and apologize but then again she would probably just blow off the sympathetic attempts and fall into a deep xanax coma she's probably already on, which she'll continue to ride for the better part of the summer now that her mind was truly fucked. There was no making this better. Nothing I could say or do would wash the images from my brain. The girl was ruined and nothing could ever change that. I cash out the tab and sway back to the car, and for some reason I am slightly more fucked than I thought but I figure this'll just put me to sleep when I get back to the apartment. I make my way right down Arlanda Street and as I attempt to drive more careful than a balancing act, I spot the car coming straight for me and it doesn't look like it's going to move out of my lane. I think *that's funny, where is he going?* Too fucked to mind, I head straight towards the vehicle and in a matter of seconds we collide head first and crush at a sudden collision that sends the other driver out the fucking windshield and into the road and my car caves in due to the weight of the other's impact. I even manage to hear a giant thud from the drivers fall as he comes crashing into the ground. I can see civilians coming out of their respective shops and restaurants tending to the body on the pavement that has found its way out of the car that flew right towards them when they were minding their own business on this quiet afternoon. I can see a family straight ahead cover up their little girl's eyes as the father is on his cell phone hopefully calling 911 even though in all actuality, he was discussing the family's next summer trip to Israel with his brother that lives overseas. I don't know how I'm still operating and where this other car even came from, but I can tell that this is bad and that by the way he was coming straight for me that this motherfucker was intending on an atrocious crash. Broken glass and red rains over my face and I can tell my head is split open from slamming into the steering wheel. His engine has somehow found its way out of his hood and onto my lap and is now sitting on my fucking thighs sizzling my legs cutting right through the denim and boiling onto my skin, and right before I pass out in agonizing pain, I hear the sirens in the distance getting closer and louder as the authorities are coming to our aid and salvation so that they can get us out of this terrible situation and just before my eyes roll to the back of my head for what would be the next seventy-two hours, I look at my phone on the passenger floor and see Angie returning my call.

THINK FAST

Right when I heard that ring tone, cool chills came down from my skull and over and out through my body and I knew it was only a matter of time before all of this spiraled into madness and that my whole cover would be completely torn apart. When I spot Darla on the floor, I scoop the hair she spat out and quickly rush outside to see if anything has changed, but the earth is still flat and no one has gone digging anything up here at this point, so that's a sign of relief. "When was Carl here?" Tara asks to which I respond a distant grumble that indicates I have no idea. She heads back to her room confused and wraps up her shower, but now I know I must act quick. I head to my room and remove my shoes, which I didn't even notice were totally covered in mud and that's when I spot the trail I left when I came in this morning. I've been turbo sloppy and know that I need to get my shit together here while Tara is still getting organized. Great, the ground hasn't been dug apart in the back and Pam's nowhere to be found. I pulled that one off flawlessly, but as I head back to my room I spot my phone and see Sam is calling in and right when I answer I can hear her talking to someone else, probably a gas station attendant she's buying cigarettes from even though she already told me she was going to quit like four times for the last five years now, and as she pulls away to her phone I hang up but it's really only a few minutes after that she calls me back and when I answer I can tell she's super freaked "did you know she was leaving?" to which I am caught off guard and don't really know how to respond and say "I don't really know how I feel about the whole thing, she didn't really go into details about anything with me," to which I realize yeah, no shit I haven't been paying attention to her at all lately, I've been to busy porking the whore I have on the other end here. "We need to talk Chuck," Sam says real convincingly and just when I think how totally twisted it would be to fuck her on a day like today even though I should probably get my head straight and make sure I took care of everything I should have, I respond "sure, how's Mika's 2:30?" then there's a pause for about two seconds and she responds "great, by the way I drove by your house earlier Chuck, your car was there, but nobody answered the door, that's real fucking classy." My skin suddenly rises from my body and I separate my thoughts from reality and fall deep into a hole, 300 feet deep, where I am left alone, speechless, breathless, and all I can see is black and all I can hear is the sound of animals fighting and a thousand bats are flapping their wings and flying away and all that's left is a distant drip of water somewhere in the background coming from the world's largest leaking faucet, and as I return to my collected self I begin realizing I might be fucked with an alibi but somehow manage to say "oh, baby come on, I don't know," thinking she's too fucking spoiled stupid to play detective. I get off the phone and put my head in my hands for a minute feeling my heart about to jump out of my chest but I manage to eventually regroup and settle. Now I just need to look around the house for a few minor details to ensure I have tied up all the loose ends before I get ready to leave here. The floor has been wiped clean and any trail of blood has been picked up when I got rid of the mud stains I left behind this morning. I go into the bathroom to clean up and shave my balls after my restless night and that shitty bus ride back on I-10. When I face the mirror, I'm too scared to look at myself but when I finally get the courage, I stare for a few solid minutes and all I can see is two deep black holes where my eyes used to rest staring right back at me and a set of fangs where my teeth used to be plugged. Absolutely terrified, I hop into the shower and see my hands have turned into two big paws and realize that I have been completely transformed into a monster and am now left to face the world in the body of a beast.

Left Alone

Cheryl couldn't believe that asshole totally blacked out when she was so ready to get her fuck on and let him have her world for the night. He seemed a bit distracted when she ran into him earlier in the night but she was totally fucking sauced when she left the house so who was she to play witness and give a rundown of what happened earlier anyway? Now that it's been a few hours since last call and about an hour into her smoking cloves out in the front porch, she's straightened out a bit and realized she made a big mistake to have gone home with junky trash. *If only I had a few girlfriends I could roll with, we would have such a ball,* but she didn't and ever since she could get on her own she's been taking her money and whoring it out on the guys, *which was fine,* she thought, it was just nights like these. *But none of that matters anyway.* As she rose up to go inside, she threw her cigarette out in the lawn by a tree that looked as if one strike of heavy wind would knock the fucker down and tear the house in half. Inside she could see Johnny, still laying on his bed face up, rubber still on his left arm and the needle laying beside him on his bed. Cheryl really doesn't care about anything at this point and realized she was going to be here all night. "Come on, just a little one," she pleas and even though he doesn't say anything when she nudges him, she can tell he hears her since his eyes have opened up to a slight degree and he is now looking in her direction. "Aww fuck it," he mumbles slightly, and striving to achieve some level of silence in the room, Johnny rises with a limp arm and a bottom lip full of saliva that drools heavily down into his lap. He reaches down and opens up a little box with a carved Indian on it that rests by his bed and pulls a bag out with what looks to Cheryl to be chalk dust and an extremely rusty spoon that looks like Johnny's been holding since he was fed Gerber as a toddler, but as he puts the two together, heats the bottom with his Sagittarius bic lighter and takes the needle from the bed and gets it full of the spoils of war resting on the stainless steel kitchenware, he recognizes the infraction of his actions but does not mind the girl's hygiene. "Tie this on and pull, then put this guy in one of those there," as he flicks his pointer finger on her forearm. As Cheryl follows suit and is excited by what the experience will hold, she quickly vanishes into a distant blip that sails with the sky and the stars and as she feels herself ooze into a million miles of oxygen and out into the stars, Johnny finds just enough strength to cook himself another shot using the same needle and the next day they wake up laying on top of one another with the plug still stuck in Johnny's arm.

THE RIDE TO MIKA'S

So I get my shit together and hop out quickly into my car avoiding any interaction with Tara and even though I can hear her calling my name in the distance as I speed off up into the road, I know she'll mind her business. Still, I know that if I don't come up with something quick or at least by the time she comes home again later I'll have to answer to her. I see her blowing up my cell and answer an affirmative *what?* to which she reminds us to leave her a copy of the key under the mat if I were planning on leaving again later on in the night. Not making any move to mind her request, I'm driving up the street not paying a minding fuck all, excited since I might get a midday when I spot a joint sitting on the floor of the passenger side. I think *this is just fucking dandy!* but right as I bend over to pick it up I slightly veer off the road and into the other lane with the oncoming traffic, and right before you know it, my face slices right up against the glass and I am left tossed out of the windshield and as I go up ten, twenty, then almost thirty feet over the other car I collide with, flying into the fucking air, I think of Pam and how much I loved her and what she meant to me and all of our good times together and how ridiculous it is for things to have turned out to be such a fucking mess and how irrelevant this particular disaster will eventually play out into the whole thing once everything blows over, and right before I crumble into the concrete I can hear Pam's laugh as if it will haunt me for the rest of eternity with the guilt and shame I will forever hold for extinguishing the flame of the one true love I have ever encountered and even though I may have been distant, this failed height brings us back down to size and as the sirens are left blaring in the background after we've slammed our head directly into the pavement, and just as I have been entirely crushed by the force the collision has provided, I shut my eyes for what feels like forever and as they make failed attempts to revive us continuously, the passers by are shoved aside and a little girl begins to cry as she asks her mother why my eyes are still open and all red and as they zip the black bag over our face and carry us into the truck bed we can almost feel a slight crack in our chest as our heart stops to beat and a cool chill is sent out through the body to declare the end of the operation.

SUMMER ROCK

I get a hold of Chuck and agree to meet him up at Mika's even though I totally hate the fucking place and their margaritas are just a bunch of sour mix dumped into a swirly rocks mug and their strawberry tossers are a punch in the face of sweetness with a shitty salt rim even though everybody knows fruit margaritas get served with sugar. He sounded rather caught off guard when I got off the phone with him, but then again he's always been a pretty distant high bastard. I do need a fuck though and I'm praying he's up for it. I figure with Pam gone and him being left alone in town he shouldn't really have an objection, but then again he's always been pretty weird about that sort of shit especially after last summer when Pam totally walked in on that threesome with Val and I, even though in Chuck's defense, she probably should've just joined us. The girl would have enjoyed herself, that's for sure, or at least it would have saved everyone the trouble of having to justify what the fuck was going on. Poor Val, I sure do miss him. I can't believe that cunt Cheryl had the fucking balls to step it up like that. Didn't really know the girl much but I did see how Val flipped a switch when they first got together once he got out of jail, cleaned his fucking act up real quick, indeed he did. I guess shanking Ben woke him up for a minute and spending time in a cell up the street from where the rest of us still partied those two summers could have the tendency to change just about anybody, and maybe it was for the best anyway, but no one really knows for sure, I guess. Sad little fucker, gone away and taken from us by some stupid skank with B+ tits. But she'll get hers someday, I suppose. Regardless, Chuck should be quite a stretch for the ol' midday even though he's a fucking wreck alright. But at the end of the day, the boy does have a fat cock and that's *for sure*, so who the hell cares, right? I get out of the house at around 2:30 and head up the street and hope that Chuck won't be pissed I'm late since I spent an extra few minutes shaving in the shower and cleaning up a few edges and didn't mind the time. As I head up to Mika's, there's awful fucking traffic. There are cars backed up all the way down the neighborhood, and I can't make that left at Arlanda to get to the bar. This is total bullshit and it's fucking hot and my AC is working like a cheap bitch and I'm getting soaking wet just sitting here behind this shitty truck that has a fucked up exhaust that continues to rattle. I pick up to dial Chuck's mobile but it goes straight to his voicemail, which drives us to fucking madness. I look ahead and try and spot the accident but can't really see anything, just a bunch of lights from the medics and police. I maneuver my way out of traffic and take a few side roads that will take me up to the other side of the street, a bit out of the way, sure, but at least I'll get some breeze instead of sitting there getting scorched to death. As I'm driving parallel to the scene down Brioche, I can see two cars in the distance in my rearview totally smashed apart and fused together, and see people rallying around the scene on the sidewalk as three more police cars come flying past me as I drive away in the other direction.

If Only's

So we sit cold again. Left alone to ourselves in our room with no one calling or wondering where we've been or how it was before we got here. Thinking of others, of everyone, of her, of them. Thinking about where everyone ended up and what they did in order for them to be able to get there. How funny the decisions they chose to follow treated them. There have been times where it hurt for us to feel this way. Silence tearing through our ears at any chance of deafening. Hours pass by, minutes tick away, thoughts scramble, and yet we are left alone thinking of everyone but ourselves and kicking over what might be and essentially, what will become. The hopeful ideals we instill within ourselves to justify the present. How we make connections within our realm in order to comprehend the way we feel. A physical relationship to a spiritual emotion. What a pathetic ordeal. We shouldn't have to crucify our efforts to enjoy our motives, instead a satisfaction of existence and connection should be sufficient, or so one would be led to believe. We make the moves and strive to achieve trusting, hoping, and believing in the idea that we will one day manage to establish ourselves in a way that seems appropriate to our standards that we have developed throughout the years. There are certain things about ourselves that we just won't ever be able to change. There are certain things that matter to us and there is no reason to explain them to anyone. Some things in our lives are unique to our personality and sense of individualism that the roots of their creation do not need to be traced or reflected upon. There are certain ways you feel when certain things happen, and there is no need to justify those emotions. There is no need to reflect heavily upon any negative emotion since it is the individual's connection with himself that justifies their behavior. At the very core, we are all romantics. We let precious love get in the way of our ability to achieve and there is no reason to hide that. However, it does get to a point where concentration deters and a way out is necessary in order to achieve successful executions of daily relationships. The bottom line, at the end of the day, and the truth of the matter is, that there is no one more for you to care for than yourself. The outsiders love you, but they can only do so much. Remember the times when you had those mental breakthroughs. They will come in use when everyone has left you behind. But I know you will continue to sit there thinking about everything you have ever done, not wondering why things aren't the way they should be, and I pray that maybe one day you will realize that you're looking for a sign of recognition that just simply isn't coming.

MEMORIAL DAY

I remember Mom making such a big deal out of it all. I mean, I sure did like the way she handled everything. She was always, I don't know, so fucking *cool* about it, I guess, that always amped myself up for some reasons just to be that way, even though I'm about five years older than she was when I can remember her being my mother. I feel sad now. I feel alone. It's been so long since I spoke with anybody, or even heard from anyone of them at all, really. It's kind of funny, not hearing from anybody even though I've only been gone a little over twenty months here and it's been about a year since I heard from Dad, from Chuck, or from anybody else for that matter. I sure do miss them though. It sure has been a while. But regardless, I feel as if everyone has entirely moved on from this whole *oh my god she's totally going to the end of the fucking world on this one* and are sort of just letting me do my own thing, you know? Of course you do, you've always been there to lend an ear to speak to. Always been there for me to explain to you just how it was that I felt towards the rest of it all, everything and to no end of it and yes, that does include the bottom end of a summer I don't completely recall but have heard the lot of it from a few of your fellies down by the local cabana. You and that cabana. A big goof you were and it saddens my heart to see you. Saddens my heart to see you this way. I always wished all the best for you. I always wished all the best.

But now there's a distance, yes, a distance, you see. But I have faith in it all, really I do. And even though right now it may seem impossible to get back to form, I know that a day will come and I will either have lived or died and to that consequence I do fulfill my obligation to inform you of my connection to the essence of everyone, to our families, to our friends, and for us to live our lives to a degree that goes written about and looked at for inspiration for years to come and gives the blind an excuse to stay bitter for we can read the words on this paper and we can see the birds in the sky. I hope like hell you're happy where you are.

REMARKABLE

SOOO we're totally fucked and I just can't *believe* that I've been dragged out of the house and am sitting HERE! Out of all fucking places! At Mika Fucking Mango's! So I'm totally out of my mind and Courtney (yes, well, *Courtney…*), is being a total fucking rave and just going off giggling about the load of the tale end of a story she's been blathering about before we got out of the car, but I'm totally cool about it since she's got a rather quirky squeak and I kind of like to hear its jingle. So there. Take it up your fucking ass and eat it, nom, nom.

Torn, I turn to the street and see that girl from the mall with the totally awesome titties that brought us out to her Christmas party from that place she worked or one of her friends worked at, fuck me I don't know, this past December. I think one of her friends got fucking shafted or something. I can't particularly recall the concrete details. But Courtney all of a sudden realizes that I'm staring off into the distance and she's like "yeah! Totally! That's the fucking chick whose friend chibbed that guy from Avandale." And as the girl walks past us she doesn't recognize me and wanders off and finds a seat inside. Courtney is a pretty cute chick with a small face and a firm posture. She rounds off with substantial tits on her short frame and proves a worthy fuck, and am interested in possibly seeing her again after she drops me off back at the apartment later to pick up the rest of my shit. I see a car pull into the lot and Courtney attempts to eyeball the driver and mouths an *oh my god* in my direction and points her left forefinger towards the driver's direction. The boy's girlfriend who stuck him and got off was rolling into Mika Fucking Mango's with Johnny T and the slight case of the fuck-all's! It was All-Out Celebrity Brawl Tuesday! No fucking Credit Check Wednesday! Who figures?

So I nod in his direction from the patio!

"Johnny!" I call, as I am totally fucking excited here! I am going for three straight days on this one and am urgently seeking more gear. The kid has the works and feels upright to nod for the social part indeed, or you could say *all* or *most* or even the MAJORITY of the night! AND can *sometimes* even cough up a buck or two your way, and I do know that if a favor indeed be asked, the boy can gather up a firm squad on a somewhat slight, yet nominal commitment.

"Holy shit boys, eh, girls," as he nods in Courtney's direction and introductions are made and that girl is just fucking standing there, totally wicked and sick looking.

"What's the fucking deal here? Rolling in with damaged goods, are you..."

I'm not even calling anyone out here just yet, but this kid was sneaking in on a dead man's girl. Something slimy about the whole thing. But she just stands there, looking, I don't know, just *awful*.

"Kyle..." Courtney elbows me in the ribs sensing Johnny's discomfort.

"What're you getting at? We're totally fucking wiped here! Catch up with me later. I'm here for the eggs," and he opens the door for the girl who looks so frail as if to combust and she stumbles in quickly, hurried to make it to the bathroom before she throws up blood all over the whole crowd and I'm still totally loose on the knob so I don't make a remark at this wild lash out here in public, but I wave it off and watch them fade in through the doors as I light a cigarette and figure I can call Johnny later if I need more shit. Courtney starts rubbing my cock underneath the table with her bare foot through my pants, and five minutes after that we're on the road and are stuck in traffic all the way from Arlanda to the other side of Khylde, but it's not too bad since Courtney continues to give us a nice firm tug job with her toes while we sit in the car.

Bourbon Bourbon

I get to Mika's and wouldn't you know it, it's totally fucking dead and Chuck's not there and needless to say he hasn't been answering any of my calls even though he did fucking tell me that he would meet me here but I figure the traffic may have got him too so I walk up the patio where a young attractive couple that I don't really seem to recognize, even though the guy is a total fuck, sit outside and they get silent for whatever reason when I walk by and open the door as I make my efforts to go inside. I hold my cell firm, and with both my hands waiting for a contact from anybody, Chuck, Pam, I don't know, and am still in a bit of a mess and also in quite a bit of a loss since it's already well into the day and I haven't heard from Pam at all. I mean, even if she was going across the country she would still have her fucking cell phone on her. I mean, get real. As I sip on my usual strawberry rita I hear a commotion behind me and when I turn around I see it's that girl who killed Val; the fucking skank with the B+ tits, and right beside her, with all his nerve and glory, the dirty rat John boy. I see him usher her way through the dining room and she looks really bad, I mean tits are still firm and nose still a knocker but she looks sick, plague-like, as if she's extremely ill, maybe hurling even, a living morgue personified, but she heads into the stall to leave and the two of us are left standing facing each other as he turns around to see me, with the sounds of her throwing up in the bathroom in the background. "*Johnny,*" I whisper and he turns around as he hears his name "what is this today, a fucking reunion..." he says under his breath, and I can tell he's caught off guard and he notices me and I look to him and ask him about Pam and he slightly chokes out "have you heard from her?" to which I nod my head from side to side and can sense that this lightweight had a little thing for Pam and can tell that he too is slightly hurt by her absence. I know I got in between the two quite a bit, but for some reason Johnny's presence never really did irk Chuck to the slightest nudge. I don't really know if the two have ever even met. Come to think of it, I don't really think they have. But here he was with some new trash fuck pickup he scooped late last night, here probably, out of all places, like all the rest of the fuckers who come into this brothel to mingle up a screw at night. The girl stumbles back out from the bathroom into one of the seats besides Johnny. I drink the entire margarita and order a glass of water. Still no sign of Chuck. I call him one more time only for it to go straight to voicemail, which is just so perfectly fucking grand now, isn't it. I drove by that fucker's house earlier and here I am again getting shit on. I personally don't need to stand for this and certainly do not need to be stood up by no disordered hippie shit-dick. I need to figure out the scoop on Pam and as I rise to leave from the table almost forgetting to pay the bill, I cause a slight embarrassment even though Johnny and the girl hardly seem to notice and for some reason am so fucking pissed I ran into this fucker, out of all people, here right now, under these conditions, but recognize that it's just not fair to bring any of that up now, since they both don't have anything to do with this. I walk down to my car and I open up the door and sit to turn the ignition on and silence the new Of Montreal release that Chuck put into my music changer, since I'm just not into that poppy shit right now. I call Pam's phone again and this time I get an error signal followed by two repeated attempts, which failed straight to voicemail, and at this point I feel so pathetic and alone and far away from everyone and anyone who has ever known me at all, that I begin to think if I ever even had the one true friend that was there for me and that's when I realize that I've always been alone and committed to bridge burning and was never really able to establish firm commitments with any one of my girlfriends when I was younger, and here I am today abandoned by the pathetic social family I have acquainted myself with and established in my life in regards to my surroundings. Right before I break into tears, I pull my strength together and call home. When the lady at the other end of the world answers and I realize it's Mom, I just want to reach into the receiver and grab her and have her hold me and tell me that everything will be alright and that she loves me and that I'm still her little girl but instead all I manage is a weak exchange that results in her having to hang up and call me back a few minutes later when I manage to calm down the nerves of my pathetic realization of loneliness and then before I zone in to her talking to me there's this giant THUD.

Walking Through The Daze

The sun is burning my forehead and this is the first thing I recognize, right before an urge to vomit my lungs out right through my rib cage making me wish I could just open up a giant chest cavity and release my organs in an efficient and sturdy fashion as well as have the necessary tools to get the burning pain that is now my every breath out from within my body, takes hold. The boy stays on the bed as I hurl over the bowl, painting the porcelain in every neon and pastel from each extreme of any art collection. But my brain now, god, my fucking brain. It's just pounding, straight, if not right through my fucking skull. God, *I think I'm dying*. God! I think I'm dying! And I suddenly just cripple and fall over on the bathroom floor and feel cold, so cold, and start shivering and am simply freaking out here and right before I black out on the cold tile, Johnny pokes us with what feel like a giant sword and places a throw blanket over me while I remain cringing in fetal position.

I wake up a few hours later, in the bed, and thankfully alone. Last thing I want to do is wake up next to anybody, especially a total stranger when I've gotten this fucked. The boy walks into the room and as he asks me how I'm feeling all I can think about is food and how hungry I am and I am practically starving and I want to go get something, anything at all to eat and for some reason the only thing I can think of is Mika Mango's even though we were just there last night and when I get up out of bed the boy refuses to let us leave, feeling for some reason a slight bit of paranoia and responsibility over the whole thing, and when I get out of bed he looks at me all weird as if I'm some kind of zombie. But in my recollection, the boy did have his shit together and took care of us firm, clean and proper and for that I thank him, even though this was a total wasteful mind fuck and he urges to escort us to get some grub and I'm down with that and even though I still feel slightly dizzy and a tad bit sick. I know I need some food and am just so fucking hungry at this point that I would eat an apple core, a pizza crust, a banana peal, straight up fucking zoo garbage even just to satisfy my needs and a little company wouldn't be half bad. We get in Johnny's car and as we drive up the street avoiding an enormous fucking car wreck that looked so bad it could have probably killed one or possibly both of the drivers, Johnny fades in and out of consciousness due to his restless nature and right before we get to the Mika's I feel like I'm going to throw up in my mouth again and when we finally pull up into Mika's, Johnny's friends are outside and I make a quick intro to which a sharp looking boy makes a snappy remark about how I look like shit and under any other circumstance I would totally claw his fucking eyes out but I feel too shitty right now for whatever reason, and I blow right past him and rush straight for the bathroom where I lose about five pounds in water and nutrients and can already recognize that something's not quite right here. When I get out of the bathroom I sit opposite to Johnny and see a girl in the room with us who looks slightly familiar. Here, sitting with us sipping on a strawberry margarita was Samantha Pranwick, the fucking slut that Val honked with his buddy. The nerve of this young slut walking into my territory! Unable to utter a word in response to Johnny's conversation development attempts, I maintain a keen eye on Sam as she orders a water and makes a fool of herself before paying her bill like a total hard-on. Right as she goes outside to get into her car I rise from the table and Johnny calls my name a few times to which I disregard his attempts to get my attention and just as she turns on her ignition I throw a giant rock I pick up at her car. The car's ignition is turned off and Sam gets out of her sedan. Just when

Sam addresses me as she gets out of the car and yells a firm and high pitched *what the fuck, bitch?* in a really slutty but almost sort of hot way that for an instant split second actually allows me to realize why Val would have wanted to fuck her, I try to swing at her face but instead all I managed to do is throw up right all over her stupid look, just oozing out blood and spoils and bleeding my fucking guts out right through my bloated red lips and I mean *all* over her face, lips, cheeks, closed eyelids, and I can even hear a slight bit of it trickle on the gravel beneath us as it drips down her chin and unto the ground and it just keeps pouring right out of me like a cartoon with XXX cans, bones and fully composed fish scales. My mouth is almost ripping at the seams off the two sides of my face, both top and bottom simply being torn apart from the pressure of all the liquid being excreted from my insides right into Sam's face and underneath her shirt and between the webbing of her toes. I feel absolutely disgusting in my illness and have no idea what is wrong with me before Johnny comes rushing outside and grabbing us and *screaming oh my god what the fuck* and I start to get dizzy again and almost fall and feel really slippery and I know I need a bed and I am feeling as if I'm going to faint but I realize that the boy knows this girl and that for some reason they may be friends but I don't really care anymore and as he apologizes to Sam on my behalf she begins to start screaming and slams the door to her car and drives away almost running us over, and right before the manager comes out and starts screaming at us to leave the premises before he's going to call the cops, I feel the boy place me into the backseat of his car where I close my eyes and the next time I awake I am alone back in my apartment laying in my bed, shivering.

V. Elements Of Disaster

MORTGAGE

I wake up by the window covered in gauze and bandages. I can already feel that half of me is gone. The accident was bad. It was so fucking bad. I don't even want to go on this way. What's the point. Should I fake it. Fake that I'm all right. So that no one will sense I am ending it. If they all know that I can't stand being this way they'll continuously monitor me. If I play the part that I am strong and capable, I will still be able to purchase the handgun as a hobby pursuit for an alibi. I am so fucking pathetic. I am not strong enough to live this way. I need to be complete. I know the other side. This is not okay, it is not all right, and there is no motherfucking talking this one through. Where the fuck is Cindy. Who even cares. Would she even want to see me this way. The last time I talked to her we weren't even on good terms. That fucking pig Savage. Whatever. None of that means shit now, anyway. I am all alone now. I stand to face the world in solidarity. There is no letting anyone get through here. Letting them get inside. This is a new me. A type of me that is missing almost fifty percent of his body. If I do go on I'll never be able to get through this. I will never be able to see the end of these fucking medical bills. Can you even begin to kid me. They say my parents will have to sell the house in order to pay for therapy. Just how fucking awful is that. As if tuition wasn't enough. My father told me the other day that my mother had quit her job so she could cash her 401k and have it distributed to her in order to pay for a series of operations that will make the right side of my face move again. They should be so very proud of their beautiful first-born son who will be able to provide nourishment for the family in the harvest season and establish a firm collection of fruits and vegetables in case of famine in one of the coldest winters ever recorded. What a terrific heir I'll make. I will fail and I am destined to be tossed over a steep edge off of one of the world's tallest mountains. If someone could just put this pathetic collection of skin and bones out of its fucking misery and turn the lights out for all eternity, I would be forever grateful. How was the other guy so fortunate to be delivered to his end, while I am left to carry the burden of that tragic day. The fucking waste of time and efforts reviving me will bring. It is so pointless and stupid now and I wish they would just give up the efforts and leave me here alone in the dark to starve.

Sick And Troubled

The wooden bead at the end of the metal switch keeps bobbing off the glass of the light. The fan is just fucking blaring and it's like, what, I don't know zero fucking degrees Celsius in this museum? I lift my head off the pillow and feel my hair stick to my face, covered in sweat. I feel awful. Like shit, actually. My stomach starts to turn and before I can even begin to remember the last thing I did before I got here, a boil bursts in my gut and I rush to the toilet and just plow my face deep into the porcelain and wretch out what is probably the better half of five or ten pounds. *What was in that shit?* I can't think about anything I've done that would make me feel half dead, but then I begin to recall that fucker Johnny, and Sam and the drugs and all that other bullshit, and I can't believe I totally hurled on that slut and what the fuck am I going to do *I just can't seem to stop throwing up* and my head spins and just before I come to rise off the floor I've been crawling on since I managed to get away from anything big enough to put my mouth in and puke into, I feel so weak and everything just spins out of control and I fade into a white sheen of light and I can feel my head hit the ground and it feels like it would probably be a really hard hit and even though I can feel the great impact of my skull cracking on the tile I simply fade, *leaking into an empty state...*

And as I think about everything, everyone, every night, all of it, not missing a single beat going through the years of laughter, struggle, pain, tears, joy, happiness, and all those birthdays and pictures and everything else and thinking of Ben, of Val, I mean I just see it all so clear and as the blood begins to outline my body laying here on the floor, I get closer to the last few days and right before I see myself outside of Mika's rushing to throw that rock on

Sam's car I feel a giant cave in my chest and as I breathe in for the last time I struggle to blow out the slightest lick of air and as my eyelids slowly begin to shut I see a pair of dirty boots come near to my face and two big paws attempt to assist me in rising and begin to pull me up off the ground but it's useless *it's useless* I say *I'm just deadweight* but the boy can't hear me and as I slip out of this shell into a state of what I guess you could call a simple essence I feel empty pathetic cold down alone simple and jealous of anyone else who has done anything in any way at all differently than me and just as I can't seem to take it anymore, I

Saw IX

So here I am showing up at Cheryl's like a fag, like I'm even into this one, but in all honesty she did get pretty sick off the shit and the last time that happened, Sam called me up from Pam's freaking the fuck out and the next thing you know Pam has gone off to New York and I'm left sitting here logging into my Brazzer's account again and who knows who this girl's friends are or what dude she's been into before she ran into my ass at the bar that could totally rip our fucking face off if he found out about some sort of skag deal. When I get to her place I light a smoke outside the apartment and ring the doorbell maybe three or four times but after about ten minutes of just standing there and ashing the cig into a plant by her door, I realize *this one ain't comin' to tha' dough yo* but I do remember the key I grabbed right by that plant I ashed in last night when I dropped her off. I put the key rock on the counter right by a few pictures straight by the ledge right when you walk in. As I walk past the kitchen not making anything out of everything, a sudden a wave of extreme panic rushes over me as I recognize the people in those photos. Cheryl, the girl that I ended up hooking up with the works the other night, is seen here with that fucker Val who fucked Sam with that kid Charles I just keep hearing about! Could this be the girl who cut the fucker? This is totally wild and as I begin to connect the pieces together one by one, soon enough I recognize why she ran out after Sam and I just have to hear this girl explain the scenario to me since I'm here first hand and you damn well know I sure do fucking want to hear it from that dirty little mouth of hers. As I walk into her room anticipating the girl to still be lopsided and sleeping I am surprised at what I discover as Cheryl is laying face up on the floor drooling with a pool of blood coming from an enormous wound in her head. I rush to the bathroom to get a towel, toilet paper, napkins, anything at all to soak this shit with or some sort of tourniquet to put pressure on the wound but everything is just covered in bile and vomit and the sink is full of blood and the toilet is smeared in every shade of brown you can just possibly imagine *I mean, what the fuck happened here?* And as I go into the room to pick her up from the floor she's simply not responding at all and as I lift her head up and try to get her into the other room it's almost as if her dead body just hurls itself away from me and onto the carpet of the den staining the rug pretty deeply and right before I grab my phone to call for an ambulance already covered in Cheryl's blood, Sam starts buzzing in.

THE WORST

I want to kill that fucking bitch! This is such horseshit! I am totally covered in fucking god knows what and who knows what the fuck is wrong with that stupid bitch anyway! I can't believe Johnny would just stand there and let that happen! Fucking standing there while the cunt throws a fucking rock at my car, what is all this shit about? I would have cut the whore's throat if I knew this would happen and I am just covered in fuck-all and all I want to do is get away as fast as fucking possible and this is just the worst fucking day of all time, like VH1's worst week ever type shit. Holy fuck. I see Mom calling but I can't answer the phone since everything, I mean EVERYTHING is just covered in vomit. This is so fucked and I'm driving like, I don't know a hundred? right down Verlanda and I just want to get the fuck away get away get away get away GET AWAY and as I pull into the complex and rush up into the flat and fly into the bathroom and turn on the shower, I am simply fuming as this tormenting stench of death just rises into my nostrils and I can't even believe that fucking happened. My tits are just covered in spunk and everything, I mean EVERYTHING and every inch of me is just loaded in this god knows what and what could possibly be wrong with the girl, I mean FUCK. Something this awful has never happened to me, *ME*, of all people. Samantha fucking Pranwick who can get any cock she wants. This is just unbelievable. It takes me a couple of hours to cool in front of the tv with a towel wrapped around my head and I'm still not over the whole thing, but somewhere around the fifth rerun of that shitty episode of Laguna Beach where Trey is going off to college and Lo and LC simply can't stop bitching about the fucking whatever it is that's bothering them this week (for some reason nobody is ever on their period on this show) I pick up to call

Johnny and tell him what the fuck and when he answers the phone
I just start going off as if it was he who threw up in my face calling
him everything from A to Z and just screaming, SCREAMING at
the top of my fucking lungs in borderline agony until I can't squeak
out another peep and after about five minutes of not hearing him
utter a single word besides the hello when he grabbed the receiver,
I drop cold when he says "Cheryl's dead," and at this I am at a total
loss as I just don't even know how to respond to that, so I hang up
and turn the tv off and go in my room to get dressed. Something's
just not right in this town and it's time for me to go home. When
I finally get a hold of Mom it isn't really a means of escape and as
exciting and cheerful as I hoped it would be as she lays it on me and
tells me how it all happened and what it was she saw on the news
earlier today.

RETURN

I want to tell Sam and explain to her that I got it all figured out and that this is the girl that fucked everyone over and started the whole damn mess between everyone and explain to her that I never knew that before right now when I just walked in here, which is funny since Sam is usually the pig that squeals and destroys any relationship worth anything between two people (at least that's my understanding of the whole thing) but she just freaks out and hangs up, which is fine. I manage to call 911 and when they get here they try to resuscitate Cheryl to no avail and it's pretty disturbing just fucking standing here while they go to work on her pumping with needles and all sorts of other shit and when they ask me "what did she take?" I just nod an affirmative no and I can hear them discussing back and forth recognizing the fact that she did not die from the impact to her head, even though the wound was enough to let oxygen into her brain to at least make her retarded for the rest of her life and I can see that they recognize the tracks on her left arm and even though she didn't necessarily over dose on the shit, she did take a pretty dirty hit and that was enough to throw her immune system in the shitter and pretty much fuck every white blood cell in her body, which is pretty ridiculous since it was me who used the needle before her and if that's the case I wonder what it is that I've got that makes people shrink and toss this way and maybe that's what happened to Pam, and before you know it they have her on a gurney and they're wheeling her away into the ambulance. It's quite awkward how they set the whole thing up, really. I thought with her being dead and everything they would at least bag her up and cover her face at least, but they don't. They lift her body up and as her head bobs, it still trickles blood down her face and down her hair, and as soon as they place her on the white sheets a red silhouette surrounds her head like a halo, and before you know it I am standing outside talking to the police about where she got the shit and even though I look like shit they don't suspect me to have done anything at all really for some strange reason, but even though they nod in agreement that I couldn't have possibly been involved in murdering this girl or taken part in any sort of foul-play, they still look at us like a sick fuck and as I stand there with all of Cheryl's neighbors just looking at this fucking scene we're causing here, my mind is just in spoils and as I space out back and forth from dreams and reality I lose my self-thought in deep, vivid waves, tornadoes, hurricanes, tsunamis, earthquakes, car crashes, explosions, destruction, pain, agony, love, loss, hate, anguish, suffering, distress, and right before I black out from this mental torture my nose starts to bleed and when one of the cops looks over as if to say *Hey! Look at him!* and recognizes this he puts me in cuffs and places me in the back of the car.

BLONDE AGAIN

I've been trying to call Neal for days now and it's really fucked how nobody told me anything at all and it takes me having to call Cindy and ask her what the fuck is going on and even though the whole deal with Savage was almost a week ago now, I can tell she's still not over it. I tell her *look bitch, some girls aren't even lucky enough to get laid,* yeah the kid's a pig but get the fuck out, check your blood, and cool it. But she doesn't even care and when she tells me about Neal in the hospital I shit, like literally, I almost shit and before you could even say one latte, please I am already in the car heading up to scoop her. When I get to her place, she's just laying on the couch in her underwear like a total bum with her feet on the table like a complete slob, looking *completely yellow* and as I yell at her to get her shit together she's just in this trance, like in fucking zombie mode and when I get by the couch and throw her feet down all she says is a nagging *"Angie…."* but I can't sympathize, fuck this girl, "get in the fucking car, *now!*" and I can tell she has no idea where we're going and as we reach the hospital, I can tell she doesn't want to be here and when we finally get the nurse to speak up and tell us where Neal's room is, we ride a silent elevator lift and as I think of Paul back in the apartment I almost throw up in my mouth a little and for some reason don't find the need or the interest at all, really to share any of these details with Cindy. We walk through the hall and get to his room. I crack the door up and I can see him sitting in his chair in the corner, facing the window. The only light comes from the cracked blinds on the other side of the room and Neal doesn't say anything even though Cindy coughs up a lung as soon as we walk into the room like a total idiot. I don't notice it at first but Neal turns around in the wheelchair and he's just fucking sitting there with a blanket over his lap. Underneath there are no legs, not even stumps, I mean this shit is just cut off above the knee past the thigh, and it's almost completely gone right up to where his cock would be leveled off right at his midsection. He sits there wearing shades. "Hi ladies," he says and I immediately begin to tear up and rush to hug him and squeeze him and he soon begins crying with me and as we're both just in this terrible sobbing hysteria and no shit he couldn't answer the phone *look at him*, Cindy just fucking stands there at the other side of the room, not moving and manages to peep a pathetic "hi neal" even though it should be her that's on her knees here, begging for his mercy, the cunt. There really isn't much to talk about in the room and before you know it we're saying our blessings and leaving and I'm still just in another world as that was probably one of the most fucked up things I have ever seen in my entire life, and as the two of us walk back into the car I am just completely disgusted with myself, my friends, my routine, my fucking hair even, all of it, I just hate EVERYTHING and I can't come to terms with this and as we ride back to Cindy's hardly saying a word, I realize I can't see Paul anymore, it's all just too awful. How could something like this happen to one of us? How could something this fucked take place to a person so innocent, to someone I knew? And come to think of it, where the fuck was Pam?

ALMOST HOME

Mom tells me all about it. She tells me about how she saw one of my friend's car smashed in from the front and how the driver flew three blocks out the windshield into the city streets. How the other driver coming from the other lost two legs in the accident and how much of a mess it created in regards to the traffic laws in this city. To this, I don't really know what to say and I sit on the bed for almost an hour, without moving. I feel absolutely torn and alone and completely fucked and now Chuck's dead in addition to Pam's disappearance. Did she know? This is just so wrong, I must have talked to the kid a few minutes right before it happened. It must have been when I was on the way to Mika's. That would explain the traffic. That would explain me sitting there for almost an hour letting my drink run while Johnny and that demon came in to borderline ruin my life. Right before I faint for I don't know, probably the fifth time this week, I take a deep breath in before trying Pam's cell phone one more time and for some reason Tara, Chuck's roommate answers to which I am completely surprised to get an answer and furiously respond "what the fuck? How do you have this phone?" and she's at a loss as to who I am at all even, and I explain and it's really only a matter of minutes before I head over back to Chuck's which is pretty disturbing since the kid totally died yesterday and here I am hanging out in his house with his roommate, but I still have to get a clarification on all of this. Pam wouldn't have left her phone behind. There simply is just no fucking way. Sure, she changed the number a few times to avoid some of the fuckers from back in high school for contacting her, but she wouldn't leave this one behind and I *know* she doesn't have the cash to get a new plan right now. I feel a serious level of anxiety completely take hold of my every move and I'm seeing spots and I'm short of breath and it's just been so difficult to even get by these last few days and everything hurts and everything's broken and I just miss, I don't know, I just miss everyone, everything, the way things used to be like, fuck man, three days ago, but there is no turning back the clock here, and I know that but I am just so sick to my stomach for all that's happened and from Cheryl to Chuck to Pam to this it's just starting to snowball like the plague and I begin to wonder if I'm next or if this is just some sick fucking plot derived by an author twisted in his demeanor with no sympathetic approach to his characters and if he can't love us, what chance does that give us in this tragically implemented fictitious plot to survive?

Downtown

They have me sitting in this room for fuck man, I don't know, like seven hours? I mean, you don't really know what time of the day it is unless you got a window when you don't have a watch and you never really take windows into consideration and how grateful you are for them, or at least should be, to be able to look out a window at any chance you get or any time you like. Finally, after enough time to let pubes sprout back unto my cock, this bald fucker comes in, a *Sgt. Davis*, and starts asking us questions about all sorts of weird shit and about where I get my gear from and where I live and why I didn't have an ID and just going up and down and every reply is as cold as an ice cube and every remark is as short as a toothpick and since I didn't have anything on me or in my car or anything at all really for them too look into, there really isn't much for them to work with here and it's really only a few minutes later that they let us off but give us an order to appear at the end of next month for driving without a license, which is totally fucked mind you, since I was in fact the one who called in for Cheryl in the first place. If I would have been there a few minutes earlier my stupid ass could have saved her from this whole deal and nobody would have really said anything and everything would have been fine and dandy. Or maybe they would've still fucked with us. After all, someone was going to worry about who was giving her the shit. Whatever man, I get to go home now and I call a cab since my car is back at Cheryl's. But god, I feel awful. I just can't stop thinking as if somehow this is all my fault, and I just feel so bad, terrible actually, and it's just inside me, this pain that's taking over my every thought and I can't even concentrate and I can't even think about anything at all besides shit, complete garbage, and how much of a fucked up person I am and how things could have been, *should* have been completely different and when did I even get caught up in the drugs and the frenzy that has been every day for the past year now and when I am laughing I'm actually crying and when I'm crying pieces of me are dying inside and it's really all the same conversion as a disorder and all this emotional instability is essentially going to lead me up to some sort of trauma and just watch, I won't even be able to get it hard anymore after all of this and it's all just madness. Simply madness, and it's actually fucking pathetic man, and it hurts, it hurts so bad, to just sit here alone in this cab ride and when I get to my car I realize I locked my keys inside it.

The Ugly's

They just came in here. They just came in here to laugh. To stare. To nod in amusement. If I am left disgusted by my existence, what hope does that even leave for them to pity me. Forget me. Repent my very presence. Don't think to invite me, to lure me into to your charms of sympathy and tragic acknowledgement. Just leave me here to die. Let time separate us and any memory you may have of our past and the way we would spend our time together. I can't compete with the outside world. I can't get in the way of what everyone is trying to achieve. My mistakes should not be imposed upon the lives of others. Do not go into efforts of trying to dig me out of this hole. I will no longer be able to be there for you as I have in the past. Those days are long ago and they are not coming back. It is with great regret that I bow down to this defeat and I hope that maybe one day I will have the necessary strength to return to you. But the beast of time will surely change things and even though our feelings for each other may be strong now, there is no guaranteeing your emotions. You do not know how you will feel towards me when I am ready to emerge. Would it even be possible for you to accept me in this form. It would not be fair to you or your future to let you know that one day I plan to see you again. You need to go. To live. To leave. To move forward. Even though it breaks my heart to sit here and watch you go I cannot be the anchor that holds you still. But they just came in here. While I sat motionless in darkness. So very still to their visit, I could hardly breathe when I smelled her at the other side of the room. It is my last day here. I am going home tomorrow. I have one more night in this place. This room. In this city. I don't know where I'll go. Sure, back home for now. But what will I do after. Is anyone even back there. Does anyone even remember us. There is no going back to the way things were, have been, or to any thought of the way I thought things could have turned out. There was no predicting this and I was not planning or ready for anything of this extreme nature to happen. I am left alone inside to die. I am left cold in here to sort through this one on my own and even though I wish I had someone to turn to and pour it on them, everything, the whole fucking short end of it and scream my failures in their stupid face, it feels liberating, refreshing and even daring to start anew.

SORTING

Tara is outside smoking a cigarette when Samantha pulls up in her Coupe blaring 3OH!3's shitty latest. Darla runs up to great Sam with a warm purr as she stops her ignition and gets out of the car. "I'm assuming you heard the latest greatest," Tara says in a sneering demeanor. The two girls had only really known each through Chuck, never really solidifying any relationship between one another. Tara heard about Sam and how she got in the way of Chuck and Pam, but fuck man, Tara's been there and knows the city limits of everyone's bikini line so she wasn't really the one to pass judgment. Sam wasn't too keen on this one either since the only thing she remembers of Tara is when she got into that altercation with Christina during Chuck's beach party when the neighbor called the cops since the girl's boyfriend was found with his cock out tugging away behind her yard to some shitty porn mag. In all respect it was a sure way to get fucked that night, but Tara just flipped the switch on this one and since it was all too rowdy to mind, all Sam recalls was Tara's attitude about the whole thing siding with the pervert who fucked her on a regular basis. *Carl*, Sam thinks his name was, and wondered if they still saw each other. Chuck mentioned something horrid about the guy before but Sam never seemed to mind the details. "Pretty fucked," Sam says, and as they head inside it's really only a few moments after that when Sam begins to interrogate and asks Tara what the *fuck* she is doing with Pam's phone. "I don't know. It was just on the counter here when it rang, so I picked it up. I haven't seen the girl over in a couple of days, I've just been working. But get this, Carl's phone was left here too and I haven't heard from him in a few either." *Carl. There it was.* But Sam was still a bit anxious. This was all too fucked. She told Tara about Pam, about the note, about

New York, and even filled her in on Johnny and Cheryl and basically broke down in front of her. "And she was just throwing up all over me and it was all so fucked and now everyone is gone and I'm all alone!" confiding in the stranger that was once Chuck's roommate and Tara is just standing *there like oh my god what the fuck is this freak's problem* since she herself maintains a resting heart rate under sixty bpm and this girl here was damn near starting to sweat, but Sam slowly beings to cool and Tara retrieve's Pam's phone from the counter and hands it to Sam and as she looks through Pam's previous calls and texts she notices that the last time Chuck had called was the afternoon the day before she disappeared and the last person to have called in was in fact Johnny T and as a ghost runs through Samantha's thin frame, she gives Tara an enormous hug and heads back in her car speeding off to Johnny's apartment almost running over Darla who is laying in the driveway catching some sun.

SOMEWHERE DOWN IN FLORIDA

Savage and Cameron pound on the bar getting the bartender's attention. It's close to two and the lights are already on showing everyone's exposed bourbon feet and pimpled faces hidden behind thick coats of blush and foundation. The night was a mediocre success as Sticky C managed to score some face from one of the guys in the bathroom and managed to rummage up an even smaller bag for the guys back out in the hall. Savage managed to scramble up a hand job in one of the booths from Briana Mason, a girl living on the outskirts of suburbia that would tease the boy every Wednesday at the student union when he walked by on his way to class. She ended up leaving early in the night, unaffected by his charms to capture her back to the house and rump, and Savage met up with Cameron and the guys who were using pitiful effects in attracting any ladies, regardless of their charming looks. The bartender turns in an affirmative reaction "if you two *fuckers* aren't going to settle down, I'll get you both thrown straight the fuck out that door, NOW WHAT DO YOU WANT?!" But Savage flashes his wicked teeth and is streamlined by the effects of the lines performed previously in the night, and then it's no problem. The boys were twisted off their gourds, rustling up the slightest bit for a tame social approach. They hadn't noticed they were banging on the bar to a point of rattling the glass it supported. The bartender acknowledges Savage's grin and gets the boys' order for two beers and a round of snake bites, in which the dickhead puts so much lime juice in the damn thing that everyone laughs after taking the shot, and someone says "for christ's sake Savage, what the fuck was that?" It's a cold night, a little oddly placed for the fading Florida fall since the summer tends to drag around the central part of the state well into late November, and maybe, if you're lucky, sometime around Thanksgiving, it starts giving in a little towards a change of season for you to take some pictures with all your cute winter shit. The cool air bursts through the room where the doorman checks id's and even though the heat of bodies in the bar supersedes the breezy chill sliding in, it is still slightly refreshing on this side of the room, but Savage simply bursts into a rage of fury and lunges out at Sticky C and knocks all the glassware off the table as he grips the throat of one of his closest friends and begins to squeeze. "Dude, what the fuck man, let him go" Cameron states in affirmation, but Savage can hardly hear him and as the guys attempt to separate Savage from his victim, Savage simply turns to them and his eyes are just encased in black and his teeth are as sharp as a razor and they're dripping saliva like a beast, all on his lower jaw and unto his button down sleeveless striped shirt, and as he chokes the life out of Sticky C, who eventually just falls over in the booth who has, at this point, turned blue and unable to get a breath of that cool air seeping in by the doorman, Savage transforms into this ogre that is unstoppable and the other guys clear the scene before explanations are necessary and as Savage is left alone with his dead friend in the booth he gains recollection and recognizes there now is a need to act quickly before the bar closes. Savage slides into the seat beside the bag of meat here and puts his arm around his shoulder and carries him out of the bar. As he walks past the guards in the front he can see them looking at him and Sticky C being dragged out like a corpse. "Too much to drink tonight," utters Savage as he walks past them, making his way back to his car. When he buckles

Sticky C into the passenger seat and gets into the car to drive away, he looks at his hands on the steering wheel after starting the ignition, dismissing his nails, which have grown over an inch throughout the course of night. Driving off, staring at the full moon in the sky and looking at the boy beside him, Savage anticipates the birth of his heir and senses the time draw near.

THE COOKIE COMPLEX

Angie sits in the living room with Paul. "It was just so fucked man, seeing him like that." It's not that Paul didn't understand where Angelica was coming from. Sure, her friend just lost his legs. That indeed was truly fucked. But at the end of the day what was there for him to do besides feel sorry for her, wished there was something he could do, and wish her friend the best and move on with his day? After all, it wasn't *his* friend; the fucker didn't even know the guy. But Angie just couldn't stop and Paul couldn't really stand having the girl cry at his place *all* day. I mean, he did have shit to do. "Look, do you want me to call one of your friends? Get them to come and sit with you? I don't really know what else you want me to do." Angie just sits there pouting like a stuck pig. "You don't understand! It's just not fair!" But at this point Paul does understand and he doesn't really give a fuck anymore and this backlash throws it all over the edge. He had a legitimate job, a respectable and fully functioning babe lair, and a good thing going for him down here and he sure as fuck didn't need this nutbag getting in the way of his weekend. "I don't know how much pouting here all day and getting pissed off at me about this is going to help you any, you can get the fuck out for all I care." It was safe to say that Paul was getting comfortable. Had this incident been a few months ago, Paul would have played the part and saw it through until its end so that he could bury his beak in some bush with the girl, sympathizing with her every detail. But after getting what he wanted for a consecutive streak here, the convenience of the whole thing started to get a bit monotonous and personally was of barely, if any interest at all to Paul here. Angie just bursts into a heavy weep and takes off and out the door slamming it behind her, leaving Paul in the kitchen sighing relief and lighting a cigarette before preparing his spaghetti and meatballs for the evening. Back in her apartment, Angelica cries for the majority of the night until she cramps up and when she goes into the kitchen to get a glass of water she decides that she won't be seeing Paul anymore and that today was the last time she was going to put herself in a position where she would need to feel sorry for herself. *I'm too pretty to be crying all day.* Even though going to the bar tonight wasn't going to be the best thing for a girl who was depressed, after feeling shitty and spending the last fourteen hours crying, she couldn't stay cooped up in the apartment by herself and she was sure as fuck not going to call Cindy to help her make things better. She was on her own on this one and she was going to see it through.

In Dreams

Water seems still enough to put our minds at ease. We are safe here. We've already been presented with the worst and now we simply float, in deep waters, fortunate enough to have each other by our side. How our love is stronger than the slightest chance of death, seeping through any slim crack between the truth, reality, and the perception of a possible future. I must say, as well as take the time to thank you, for always being there and being honest. The truth has not been pretty and it certainly has not been an easy one to speak of. But you were there with me and I was there as well and I am in a rational position to be able to understand your primary, although childish, current concerns. So now that we have been there, and now that it has been some time between the acts of love and reflection, *this* is how you feel? At this point, and by now at least, believe me, I could have sworn we were past the trivial. But we're not, and *this* is what you come up with? And as I sit here talking with you and completely understand where you are coming from and recognizing that all of your concerns are completely legitimate ones, I simply cannot believe you find *now* to be the time to discuss them. I understand I have been bad. Do not attempt to infuse your ideals of yourself and how you reacted in comparison. They are no match for my past behavior. I certainly was no saint, and for that I do apologize. But in the distant rear, did we not already discuss this? Are we not bigger men and women who are able to shift our scope and recognize that change is possible? Has society shifted our hope in mankind to such a degree where one does not believe the person they love can change for a common good? Have our times designed rules and guidelines that define how we will feel no matter what changes take place? Can the deception be traced to our schools? Or is it our government? The advertising, the concessions, all of it. Has every inch of it been predetermined to our actions (that are just, *oh*, so predictable!) when change affects us? How will we ever be able to grow? At this rate, are we even capable of truly feeling the ideal? Is what we think to be love merely a shallow framework that is essentially webbed seamlessly between two people and begging for a rock to be tossed within itself so that it could crumble? You should know by now as we drift away, slowly in a calm and soothing fashion in two completely separate directions, that although you seem confused about what lies before you, deep down inside you know how you should handle this but are just too scared and afraid of being responsible to be able to handle and nurture the gift you have been given. In dreams, I could speak to you in confidence. In dreams, I could rely on the comfort you had provided. In dreams, I could feel warm and safe in the closure your friendship brought me. But no longer is any of this possible. Use your efforts to deny this and do not accept my love. In dreams, I see you sailing far away from me tonight, knowing that you are not fair.

SUBTLETIES

Johnny gets in the car and just drives and fades, unable to cope with the connections between everyone and when he gets back to the apartment he's excited and feels good to meet Sam who immediately begins to accuse him of everything from getting in the middle of her and Pam and the whole god damn relationship from top to bottom and just before Sam begins to nauseate over the concept of what it is they are even discussing here she just shuts up and Johnny just fucking stands there, licking the boot. "It's not like I'm sitting here happy with the way things are," but she can't hear him. She's deaf to his excuses. Sam too, has faded. There is no life in these few any longer. There is nothing left for them to comingle. They have used up their welcome and are no longer even convinced to be in the middle of anything. Their rational is twisted and they are committed to believe that they are not welcome. Although, in all reality, there is nowhere for them to go. The combination of their relationships and what it was they did that brought them all to get here essentially tore down the communication between them and any sort of connection with the real world. They have crossed the line into the next few words that will bring them to their end and at this point, am convinced it can be said without repair. Sam has indeed come full circle. This is a confirmation of the affirmation that indicates that we all have closure on the events that happened here today. At this moment, we are here by expecting a firm decision on how it is that you feel about all of this. After all, your judgment will weigh plenty. As you see, you have read the tale of the unfolding and molding and schmoozing and the oozing and the boozing and the destruction of the heart the soul the love the torment and pain and agony and everything else in between that it had to do with, while you just sat there and read all about it and as it quickly progressed you realized there was just no way out no way out now way out for anyone and that even though it managed to establish itself to some sort of something you may have seemed to recognize, in the end you convinced yourself that you could simply just not relate and that this had nothing to do with you all along. By the time the witness has been called to sanction the seal on the entire case, the Wrangler, the blonde, and the vampires will have all filled in a slot to mingle and be brought about to boil as the ripping film melts away and the reel is left slapping around a piece of plastic that revolves repeatedly rotating over the projector until Courtney, two hours into her shift, turns off the switch.

VI. Before The End Is Carried

CRYSTALLIZED

The pink H3 is cruising on the streets again and Cindy has her windows rolled down and as her hair blows in various directions, she turns down the blaring system before tying the blonde back in a bun. It is a fairly cool day, the sky is clear and the sun is just about getting ready to set. Her stomach has been absolutely destroying the inner sides of her tubing, and she feels as if her lips down below have fattened up a bit. Regardless, Neal's mother had called Cindy to have her pick up Neal's Wrangler from the apartment and drive it back so his father could drive it down to the house out in Boca. Cindy felt sick. She felt distant and empty and absent and not the freshest batch of apples or a cool hit of the daily crip was going to sort this one through. Time would heal this, she figured. That's all it would take. But just how long would have to pass for her to distance this disaster from her general conceptions of the world around her? How would these events impact the way Cindy approached her everyday interactions and future progressions and attempts at love? Surely, our sweet and slightly poor Cindy here, was an emotional nightmare. A roller coaster. A faded trend. A daily value. A weak attempt at triumph. *I should have become a model* she thinks but realizes she's already one year into her twenties and the girls usually start when they're twelve, and besides, she just wouldn't fit in with that crowd anyway nor did she even have the work ethic to be anything more than a dirty stamp licker. Complicated. It was a fucked up deal and a shitty hand that was given to this one, that's for sure. At the apartment, Neal's mother stands outside waiting by the Wrangler. "Thank you so much for doing this, I know you're going out of your way, but there was no way we were going to pull this off without a third person, and Neal, well, it's not like he can really operate a car right now," all the while her lips are staggering, holding back a floodgate of tears and this makes Cindy cringe in a slight agony and she immediately pushed the image of Neal in the hospital, sitting in the dark, to the back of her mind. "It's absolutely no problem, anything I can do to help. I know it must be really hard for all of you right now," but she didn't care about this young cunt's sympathetic appeal or slight bit of regard for her family, and she quickly molded into this new banshee demon that spawned from hell as she squinted her eyes and grabbed Cindy by the arm and spit out "I know how you girls like to fuck around and could care less about emotions and all that, and revolve your ideals around your exploited and purging labia's, but not my Neal sweetheart, you just don't fuck around with my family," and Cindy is caught standing still not knowing what to say. Should she just leave? How should she handle this situation? *How dare this bitch speak to us this way* and right before Cindy lifts her arm to swing in her direction she hears that voice "*Cindy,*" and just before she passes out in the road in the middle of the complex she gains her composure and manages to formulate a weak "*I'm so sorry, Neal.* I am *so* sorry" but she should know by now that her apology is days too late and as Neal sits there, rolling slowly towards her in his chair, he thanks her for helping him through all of this, for whatever reason really, being overly distant and nonchalant about any of their past endeavors or connections and relationships. Cindy can feel shingles fall inside her and as her heart breaks into a thousand pieces as she watches him legless, forcefully spinning the wheels of his chair, she takes the keys to the Wrangler from his mother's hand and drives the car to the Budget where his dad is waiting for her to drop off the car. It's a complete silent drive back to the complex and Cindy can tell that Neal has told his parents *everything* and Cindy recognizes the confidence she thought she had with an acquainted love has been dismantled when faced with adversity and that even though ultimate comfort can bring out the honest truth between two people, it is safe to never share all you got. When they get back to the complex, Neal and his mother are already gone and right before Cindy gets out of the Wrangler, her stomach is in an ultimate cramp. She apologizes one last time to his father but he just looks straight ahead holding the steering wheel 10-2 and drives away not a second after she shuts the door, almost running over her newly pedied foot.

TROUBLES AT THE MOVIE THEATRE POOL

I'm just laying out in the front lawn at the house and some of the new girls have been coming and going and coming and saying hi but I'm totally zonked so I don't really do much more than wave or make the slightest smirk. The strawberry fruit passion I brought out has completely melted and turned into a steaming cup of sugar and as I rise and go inside to get a glass of water, my suit totally sticks to my chair and just when I notice that half my ass is hanging out of my bottoms these two boys who don't look to be too much of a threat come by on their bicycles eyeing the fuck out of us, which is fine, but when they come up and start talking to us about the weekend and what we're doing later is enough to get me to rush in through the doors and when I get into the kitchen one of the girls is sitting at the table just going off to her boyfriend on her cell phone and she is just screaming and crying and getting so upset that it's actually quite disturbing and I can tell that deep down she doesn't want to leave this guy and even though she is making it very clear to him that she doesn't ever want to see him again and doesn't care whether he comes and visits her this weekend or next weekend or homecoming or for the game or ever at all for that matter and that she is just fucking over it, I can tell that deep down she doesn't want to be saying this, and that she loves him and that everything she told her friends and all they talked about eventually was building up to this and that this is what she came up with after thinking very thoroughly about how she felt about the whole thing and now that she is here with plenty of time on her hands to get into it and get everything sorted out and finally talk to him about the whole deal and the way she feels, she is just going to throw it all the fuck away and after all the time she has put into this she no longer wants him to be a part of her and she does not ever want to talk to this guy again and even though she might realize somewhere down the line that you do not treat people this way, right now she doesn't want to have anything to do with it and I think, *how terribly sad.* It is possible to get so upset that you will throw everyone around you away. It is important to recognize that these emotions will pass and that everything will be all right. I take a shower and watch a new Treehouse of Horror special and the whole *Maggie's never really gonna talk on this show thing* really isn't all that funny anymore. I decide I should probably call Paul a little later in the night and when he answers he isn't too excited to hear us and when I think about the girl from earlier in the afternoon I just kinda get turned off the whole thing and when he asks us what we're doing later I sit silent for about two seconds and it's only a few moments after he calls my name several times that I just hang up the phone and watch it ring repeatedly on the counter for the next hour and as I pull the covers over my head, I can still hear the phone vibrate until it falls off into a pile of clothes that's down by the dresser.

No Respect For The Dead

The lips of earth that ate the fallen and those who have past away have crumb remains within their whiskers. A global sight in aerial view handed out to passers by. Everyone will know what everything looks like. This is conducting business in the daylight. A torch for the visitors, and a pitchfork for those familiar with the band. These men are good, for they know our chant. There is a curtain, which would certainly indicate that there has to be a show. But the lights are dim and the dancers have fallen, on what degree do we exist? Are we in the middle of some show where the likes of us just fade in and out within each season? Where are the burials in all of this? The ceremonies? The bills, the licenses, jurisdiction, the whole lot? Fucking hell, where are the parents? Isn't there anyone to report this claim to? A claim for one to indicate perhaps?

Soothe me so that I'll understand, baby...
Soothe me so I'll understand...

So we begin to go ahead, without certain pleasures, but ahead no less, proceeding further. To those of which we have offended, please do not be so mindful that this was an intent to harm you, for we have been hurt as well. The connections we have established throughout the course of this exchange can never be reversed and you are forever affected by my connection with you. Like those friends in your past that I became oh so familiar with years down the line, I too have made a staple in your existence. Remember me, for I have taught you well. I have taken the time to listen and formulate thoughts with you. The rest, well, the few are legless and several are colder than ever, but in the end everyone leaves walking away with that special something and whether it be more or less depends on the individual, but the bottom line is that you can't say we didn't leave our mark to be by your side. We strive to continue to make decisions that we hope and think will benefit us and our community. The people who we love and are closest to us. The people that we are able to trust. We make decisions that we hope will better every aspect of our lives on a daily basis and bring happiness into our hearts and our families. We continue to remember and praise those of which were once amongst us who are no longer, and even though we continue to grow and move forward without them (those of which have changed us ever so drastically) we keep them close to our hearts knowing that one day we will all be together again.

Banana Nana

In line waiting for a mocha I ordered, which has been taking a surprisingly long time to make even though the place isn't really all that busy, I stand weighing heavily on my right leg. But it's okay though, since I'm currently spotting this wickedly hot guy checking out my tits in this skinny pink top, and even though I make eye contact with him like, I don't know, three or four five six seven eight nine times maybe, does he actually come up to me and say "so *hey*, is that a latte?" and when I reply he asks me about my boyfriend to which I laugh and he asks if he could join me even though I tell him "I'm just getting a quick sip to go," but god, this guy is just so gorgeous, and I'd be damned if I didn't even make an attempt to fuck him. With Neal and all, sure I felt bad, but I couldn't just stop thinking about myself, could I? I know I've felt low before but I just need this one. *I need to move on.* I get the boy's number and he says his name is Kyle and when I tell him I'll catch up with him later I can tell he doesn't believe that I will and later on that night when the girls are all getting ready to go out and Angie is still not answering her phone out there in her apartment somewhere, I call Kyle and he eagerly picks up and I can hear some commotion in the background, and he strikes me as the kind of guy who knows where it's going on. Like he knows what the deal is, *at least most of the time*, and I could use that. I could use some assertiveness around here and he's good looking enough to have around. I get off the phone feeling a slight cramp in my lower stomach, like I felt when I had that pump after Neal fucked me that one time and didn't pull out. It was shitty waking up hungover the day of the appointment and going to the clinic to get flushed out after I missed my period. It gets a little scary, especially when you can't make the first appointment

they try to schedule. When you ask for a later date after their first
proposition they get silent for a brief moment, and you're thinking,
and the person on the other end is thinking and everyone's passing
judgment and you slightly laugh to yourself since after all the whole
thing does require some sort of consideration and practice of time
deepening in your daily schedule. We meet Kyle at Mika's where he
shows up with four of his other buddies, all very good looking mind
you, and I introduce them to some of the new girls from last fall's
pledge class that drove us all out here and they're buying us drinks
and some of the girls are out dancing with the guys already and it's
really only a few minutes after midnight that Kyle and I are already
making out by the Tiki bar in the back of the patio, and right before
he lifts my skirt up and starts to get me real wet inserting first two
then three then four and finally his whole fist deep between my legs,
I feel another tight cramp that causes us to cringe so quick and hard
that Kyle has to make sure we're all right and when I tell him I'm
fine, he keeps kissing us, but when I tell him to stop he doesn't and
it's then that I start trying to force him off me but he keeps making
further advances and I suddenly get so scared that I just tighten up
and go right back to that night where I'm fucked out of my mind
*and now it's mountains oozing blood lightning cracks the sky big beasts
fly above in an orange sky breathing fire spitting chewed bones of those
fallen to their grasp and prey and just as I look into the eyes of the demon
on that one fucked up night when I left Neal.*
Neal...
No...
and they were all just watching and when I scream real loud and snap
back to Mika's, Kyle is just standing there, but he's about three feet
back now asking if I'm alright. "Let's go back inside," and I grab his
hand and escort him inside where the other girls are now sauced with

dancing. My cramps become unbearable throughout the night, and I feel bad when Kyle asks us to dance and I just make a pathetic effort to smile that is essentially overshadowed by my enormous grinning frown caused by the pain in my lower stomach. Right before last call, I excuse myself and make my way into the bathroom and crawl into a stall and sit on the bowl and put my feet up on the seat and put my head down between my knees and for some reason, just start to cry and my head hurts from all these blackouts and these thoughts *these crazy fucking thoughts* and I'm pouring and raining tears and I'm just bawling and I can feel pain. Deep, sharp, stinging pain, and it hurts and it just feels so awful, like something is biting me, like teeth are inside my stomach, ripping apart from my intestines, both small then large respectively, and slowly making their way throughout my entire body going through my lungs and up through my throat and I can feel that gagging reflex just before you know you're going to puke and feel extreme relief and right before I do and feel pressure on my tongue going all the way down my neck, my mouth suddenly is forced open and I see what appears to be a giant sack being formed from between my lips, tearing apart my fucking jaw as if I am chewing a giant piece of gum blowing up a black bubble that continues to grow and grow and grow to a point where it's about to erupt from my insides, just getting bigger and bigger and I look like a frog croaking on a lily pad and I can tell I am about to be fucking ripped in half here and this appears to be some sort of birth giving procedure to some other creature. *This is no human baby* and right before I have this realization that I will not survive this and proceed to black out from the agony *duh what human baby is born out of your mouth pretty blonde* the giant bubble grows so large and it's now bouncing up and down that it bursts into the next stall as my head cannot support the giant cyst. The weight causes it to break through the room and a few of the other girls just start screaming, running out of the bathroom and I can hear their heels click on the tile as they rush out the door trying not to slip, and right before the bubble erupts and there is just puss and blood all across the room and this little purple demon baby thing no bigger than two feet max is rising from inside the rupture making a creaking sound and screeching, he walks into the ladies room and I just completely freeze laying there twitching on the wet bathroom floor with my bottom jaw completely ripped off. Savage, surprisingly well-groomed, wearing a dark overcoat and black slacks, bolts through the bathroom and picks up the demon baby right then and there with all the blood covering his big monster hands with nails that have got to be longer than a few inches. Suddenly what appear to be two enormous wings spread and cast an eclipse over the light glaring in my face. Savage flies away into the orange night sky, leaving the entire bar staring up at his ability to do so. He is off into the darkness stealing the beast that just erupted from within me and has torn my face apart. It isn't too much longer thereafter that I shake for a final time and simply lose too much blood to carry on.

The Terrible Misfortune Of Being Blind

I find it totally dick that Chuck's stupid bitch friend told me she was going to stop by and just had me sitting here all fucking day waiting for her to get here. *Stopping by and storming out the way she did.* She seemed nice enough, but fuck man, I would have went out and caught that new Will Ferrell movie that just came out on Friday, the one based off that old tv show where they go back in time and fight off dinosaurs and shit. If only I knew she wasn't going to stay for too long. That would have been pretty cool I imagine, and maybe Carl would have wanted to come, I don't know. She sure sounded worried though, so I figured giving her the respect to talk about the whole thing was only fair. Whatever man. So I go outside and let Darla out and she quickly hops on this mound of dirt out in the yard. It's funny actually, I've never noticed what a damn mess the backyard is. I've lived here for a little while now, well not too long, but long enough to need to know what my own fucking backyard looks like. Maybe I should straighten some of this shit out. Chuck was a real outgoing guy, sure, but he wouldn't take the initiative to get the lawn organized. What was I going to do with the house now anyway? Would I still be able to live here now that the landlord was dead? Who knows. Nothing like some yard work to get the mind off this wild nonsense, as Mom always said. The neighborhood lawn maintenance tidies up the grass, but this backyard just looks like a fucking war zone. Like the *Don't Tell Mom The Babysitter's Dead* lawn. I figure I'll head up to Rick's and grab some decent flowers from their landscaping den. You'd think they would have some cheap shit, but when I get there they're charging like $35.60 for a sheet of anything, and everything is being sold in bulk and fuck man, it's just going to be too much money and just *way* too much work. I end up buying a few different types of spring lawn flowers and figure the purple ground ivy will be useful for a slight mint aroma, while the few patches of strawberry flowers with the yellow centers will prove to be very soothing and bloom efficiently around this time of year. It doesn't really ever get *that* cold in Florida, anyway. When I get back to the house, I place the flowers on the porch table and go grab the shovel that's right by the big dirt mound I noticed earlier. I figure this will be a prefect place to start since it already looks like shit, it's in the middle of the yard, and is the first thing people will look at when they walk back here and instead of saying "holy shit, what the fuck is that thing?" they'll be pleased to be greeted by fresh batches of blooming petals. Surely these too will die, but for now it's a great way to clean this shit up back here and since I guess that cunt isn't planning on coming back over here any time soon, it's a hell of a way to kill the rest of the afternoon. Right as I stick the shovel into the dirt mound there seems to be a slight resistance, as if I seem to have struck something deep within the ground. Only about half the shovel is in the ground, but I figure I'll just dig around it, thinking maybe it's a root that was left behind by an old stump that may have been here when the previous owners lived here maybe. But as I keep digging and digging the thing in the ground doesn't seem to be a plant or any type of wood or root for that matter. There seems to be a circular object here, like it's a piece of metal or glass or something, and that someone has buried this thing here in our backyard without making much of an effort to hide it. I hit the top of the object a few times and it clicks the shovel and it sounds as if I'm tapping metal on metal. I keep digging around it and it's really only few moments before I dig about two feet into the ground that I realize that *holy shit it's a human head* and just when I begin to conceptualize what it actually means to me in my backyard and who these people are,

I notice that there are dirt mounds just like this one all over the yard, five, six, seven, eight, nine, ten of them, I count. Right about the time where I fall on the grass trying not to swallow my vomit due to my loss of breath, not knowing what to do, I see Darla begin hopping from mound to mound digging in with her two front paws deep, getting dirt all over her orange fur.

BE WATER

Dad always said family was everything. I'll never forget standing outside in the driveway waiting to get in the car with all of our shit packed trying to slide away to make the journey back home. He told us that this is what counts. Family. And then he said it again, and kept on making hand gestures that expressed unity, closure, and trust. Us having each other, he said. That was all we needed. He said that as long as we had family, everything was okay. Everything else was bullshit. Or so he believed. It was at that moment that I don't think I ever felt more alone. I was thinking of everyone. My friends, my fucks, all the dates, teachers, servers, republicans, every girl I've kissed, every boss I stole from. And sure, I was thinking about my parents too, and let's not forget all my siblings. After all, we were a rather large family who were in fact, all generally good people. But I always wanted to establish a bond, or some sort of connection with someone who wasn't forced to like me. Family sticks together. Sure. As long as you don't steal from your parents account and commit fraud under their alias or disgrace the family name or shoot someone, then why would they not have the desire to accept you? Even parents who find their children to be complete losers, drug addicts, molesters, and violent offenders still provide them shelter, warmth, love and compassion in their time of need and let them sleep in their guest room or couch for months if they need to. Lions roll with other lions. Of course it's fucking pathetic, but that is what family is there for. I always thought differently. I always believed that as long as I had myself, I would be all right. I do not need family for I have something better. Again, I have myself. I am the one who is best suited to answer all my questions. I am the one most fit to determine what is best for me. Any discussion with anybody else concerning what it is they think I should do is a wasteful use of both time and words, or just another opinion of an option I won't consider. There is no logical insight you could possibly provide me to the way I currently manage my existence. All of your ideas and comments are somehow linked to an emotional appeal or connection that has somehow influenced your past and your future decision-making. If I were to discuss something that is so very real and concrete to me, those emotions you have towards your ideals might strike an argument and essentially make me behave and explain myself in an irrational fashion. When I speak, I speak unbiased. So do not lure me into your pathetic attempts to strike an argument. My attempts in life are only trials to find out what is best suited for the next situation. Determining which conditions would be the proper fit for me, and lurking in the corners of this world when necessary. When I do what you like to consider mistakes, recognize that I am the one learning through the experience and you are simply there, passing judgment on my behavior and new experiences that you will never get the opportunity to live through. Just who exactly is gaining anything from this dilemma? Would I go as far to say that this makes me the better person? Or are you the guided light sent here to navigate me through the pathways of life? I always respected Dad for giving us that unconditional love and placing us in his web of trust and I certainly do appreciate the fact that he considers our presence to be such a crucial asset, however I still know that it is me who has to sleep with the decisions I have made, and it is me who wakes in the morning each day and has to face the consequences of my actions and it is me who has to stare deeply alone into my own reflection and go down the crossroad that I chose. Thank you so much for your kind consideration, but I will have to excuse myself out of this union. For time cannot change me, since only I can change myself.

Prey On Life

The midnight air is cool and a slight mist is felt all around me at this elevation. High enough up above, but still low enough to see the light resonate from all the cars. Down there, heavily flowing into steady traffic. It is a full moon and the sky is clear enough tonight where you can spot the craters just right to be able to gauge depth perception. I can feel my wings weigh in pressure from the gusts of wind that are rising from beneath me. As I make my way through the city, I can finally take some time to organize my thoughts and calm my senses. It will be great to bring the young into the household and establish a new relationship with Susana. It's a real shame that she can't play the part, but I guess I still have the ability to take matters into my own hands. We will treat this one right. Not like those in previous millennia's, which either ran off or died. We will make this effort be the one that counts for the Silothian legacy. Certainly the chase of finding a proper host has always been a blast, but how much longer before they finally find us and stick the fucking daggers through? How much longer can we continue to migrate from city to city starting over all the time? Poor Cindy though, she didn't take it anywhere near as well as the others. Not that they survived (nobody *ever* survives) but this was just a little more wet than usual. There was just blood everywhere. It could have been from the seat that broke in there when she burst, after all, porcelain was covering the *entire* floor. But it's okay, we won't have to worry about her or Cameron, or Sticky C or any of those fuckers anymore. We can move forward with one. I look underneath my wing and see the little one curled into a ball, attempting to shun from the windy chills the midnight air provides. I bring him closer to my chest and go about 1,000 feet lower in elevation where the temperature is a bit warmer.

I am sure Susana doesn't like it the slightest bit either. Her jealousy issue when it comes to these rituals goes through the fucking roof. I like to place enough time between each attempt to let her blow the whole thing over, but I've tried to explain it to her over and over again, *we're animals honey, it's what we do* but she never seems to mind the slightest bit. It's not my fault she fucked around once too many with different breeds, fucking up her guts. You don't see me using that against her, and now we're starting new with this one and we will make it work. As I glide into the balcony of the complex and make my way down the emergency stairs into the building, I walk slowly back to the apartment feeling slightly awkward about the whole thing and feeling a bit spacey. I look forward to seeing Susana and laying next to her and feel confident in knowing that all of this is going to be entirely beneath me in the morning. When I open up the apartment door and place junior in the bed Susana and I set up for him months ago when we decorated his room, I call out for her name, but surprisingly, she is not here.